BRUNHILD

THE DRAGONSLAYER

Yuiko Agarizaki
Illustration by **Aoaso**

Brunhild's is a strange and cruel fate.
Born of dragonslayers,
she was raised the daughter of a dragon.

BRUNHILD
THE DRAGONSLAYER
CONTENTS

Illustration: Aoaso
Original Cover Design: Shunya Fujita (Kusano Design)
Yen Press Cover Design: Eddy Mingki

The days passed by, and she grew from a toddler into a young girl.

And as she grew, her hair changed color from jet black... to silver.

THE DRAGONSLAYER

BRUNHILD

Yuiko Agarizaki

YEN
ON
New York

BRUNHILD
THE DRAGONSLAYER

Yuiko Agarizaki

Translation by Jennifer Ward

RYUGOROSHI NO BRUNHILD
©Yuiko Agarizaki 2022
Edited by Dengeki Bunko
First published in Japan in 2022 by KADOKAWA CORPORATION, Tokyo.
English translation rights arranged with KADOKAWA CORPORATION, Tokyo, through Tuttle-Mori
Agency, Inc., Tokyo.

English translation © 2024 by Yen Press, LLC

Yen On
150 West 30th Street, 19th Floor
New York, NY 10001

Visit us at yenpress.com † facebook.com/yenpress † twitter.com/yenpress
† yenpress.tumblr.com † instagram.com/yenpress

First Yen On Edition: May 2024
Edited by Yen On Editorial: Payton Campbell
Designed by Yen Press Design: Eddy Mingki

Yen On is an imprint of Yen Press, LLC.
The Yen On name and logo are trademarks of Yen Press, LLC.

Library of Congress Cataloging-in-Publication Data
Names: Agarizaki, Yuiko, author. | Aoaso, illustrator. |
Ward, Jennifer, translator.
Title: Brunhild the dragonslayer / Yuiko Agarizaki ; illustration by Aoaso ; translation by Jennifer Ward.
Other titles: Ryuugoroshi no Brunhild. English
Description: First Yen On edtion. | New York, NY : Yen On, 2024–
Identifiers: LCCN 2023057875 | ISBN 9781975378929 (v. 1 ; hardcover)
Subjects: CYAC: Fantasy. | LCGFT: Fantasy fiction. | Light novels.
LC record available at https://lccn.loc.gov/2023057875

ISBNs: 978-1-9753-7892-9 (hardcover)
978-1-9753-7895-0 (ebook)

10 9 8 7 6 5 4 3 2 1

LSC-C

Printed in the United States of America

Prologue

A violent storm tore through the quiet of the night. Such weather was unusual for this place.

The raindrops striking the window glass were as loud as machine-gun fire. The howling wind was so turbulent it threatened to reduce the man's simple home to rubble.

He was alone in his hut.

The dark glass of the window poorly reflected his visage. He appeared to be in his thirties, though his hair was stark white. His robe, a similar shade of white, bore an antiquated pattern.

His eyes were an icy blue.

The humble room was adorned with simple furniture and illuminated by the warm glow of hearthfire.

The man sat on a stool before a half-finished painting.

His gaze shifted to the window, but it was pitch-black outside. He couldn't see a thing. The heavy rain, the dark of night, and the shaded glass made for the perfect storm.

But the man continued to stare out the window. He wasn't as concerned with what he could and couldn't see. The mere act of looking out the window was enough to fuel his creative process—it gave him the power to imagine.

Upon the canvas, he had painted a sunny sky over a grassy field—and a girl standing at the center in an unsullied white dress.

His brush hand worked tirelessly. It was as if his eyes truly beheld the girl in the grassy field through the window.

Then there came a loud bang.

Something had crashed into the glass.

Something red.

At first, he thought the window had been hit with a torrent of blood. But upon closer inspection, it was a woman.

A woman in a red military uniform had leaped into view from the edge of the window.

All at once, time seemed to stand still.

I could never mistake that. Not me…

The woman's mouth flapped open and closed. It seemed she was saying something, but her words were drowned out by the forceful wind and never made it to the man's ears.

There came another loud bang.

The woman slammed into the window again.

Time flowed once more.

The woman was demanding to be let in.

Oh God, may I invite her into this hut?

A moment later, the man went to the door.

Seeing him move finally, the woman also raced toward the front door.

It was a struggle to open the door. The wind outside was so brutal it was as if the hand of God was forcing it closed.

Once the door was cracked open enough for a person to slip through, the woman tumbled inside. A deluge of rain came in with her, nearly soaking the man's clothes.

"Sorry. Thanks." The woman pushed back her wet bangs.

She appeared to be in her late teens. Her glossy silver hair drew the eye. When it swayed, glittering droplets scattered this way and that.

She was pale beyond comparison. It was as though the very concept of pigment was alien to her. It had to be because she'd just been out in the wind and rain. Her lips were turning purplish.

But her eyes were red.

<I knocked on the door several times, but it didn't seem like you

could hear me. I knew it was rude, but I had no choice but to start banging on your window,> she said.

Examining the woman's military uniform, the man said, <Soldiers aren't common around here,> as if he didn't know the woman at all.

With a troubled smile, the woman replied, <I'm sure.>

<I'll get you something to wipe yourself off with. Wait in the room with the hearth.>

The woman thanked him.

The man returned to the fireplace room carrying two sheets of linen cloth. The woman had taken off her uniform and was sitting on the rug in front of the fireplace. Her deep-red uniform, made of high-class cashmere fabric, had been abandoned like a snake's shed skin.

She wore a lace camisole. The light of the fire dyed her hair a brilliant crimson. Her lips had also changed from purple back to a healthy pink.

She smiled at the man. <Sorry again for being so indecent. You'll have to forgive me. My uniform was soaked through, and it was sticking to my skin most unpleasantly. It was heavy, too. Being ceremonial, it has a lot of decorations.>

Handing over the linen cloth, the man said, <I don't mind, but it would be best not to expose yourself like this in the house of other men. Lust and desire are sins, after all. You don't want to seduce a man and go to hell, do you?>

<Oh, you don't have to worry about that. I'm going to hell, lustful endeavors or no.>

<Because you're a soldier?>

<Yes. I've killed many. I've manipulated men, too. And on top of that...>

...On top of that, I'm a dragonslayer.

The man's blue eyes widened. <...You're a dragonslayer.>

<I was quite famous for it in the Norvelland Empire. My name is Brunhild Siegfried.>

<Sorry, I'm not familiar with the name.>

What the woman—Brunhild—said was true. The house of Siegfried was an old and respected clan of dragonslayers, and Brunhild herself was also famous for her noteworthy accomplishments in battle.

It was just that the man had lived in total isolation. On sunny days, the man had spent his time picking fruit, playing with animals, and talking to flowers.

<Well, it's no wonder you wouldn't know.> Brunhild gave another awkward smile. It didn't come across that she was scoffing at the man for his ignorance. <Will the rain let up once the sun rises?> she asked.

<Only God knows,> said the man. Living so far away from civilization, his spirituality was different from that of ordinary folk. <It was by the grace of God that you were able to come here, as well. God has allowed you to come to this hut and warm yourself.> He pulled the stool close to himself and sat down. And then after a moment's pause, he said, <If you don't mind, could you tell me your story?>

The man looked at his canvas. The room was decorated with many paintings the man had made. All of them bore the motif of bright scenery and a girl in white. <If I hear your story, I might be able to paint something better.>

Seeing the girl in the painting, the woman said, <Could this girl be...> She was very good at reading people's hearts. <...your...?> She changed her mind, adopting a softer lilt in her speech.

<Mm-hmm. You look like my daughter,> the man replied.

The woman lowered her long eyelashes. <I look like her? In other words—>

<Ah-ha-ha, no, no. I'm sure she's still alive out there, somewhere. Though, wherever she is, I hope she's not wearing a military uniform. I don't want her to be in such a bloody profession,> said the man.

And he said this even while knowing who this woman really was. Who could say if this was a religion-based criticism or his vain struggle against acknowledging the truth in front of him.

Silence.

The soldier didn't know how to respond...

...and the man did not continue.

<The only story I have is a bloody one... You don't mind, do you?>

<If that's all you have, then so be it.>

The woman was silent for a while, but eventually she opened her mouth as if she'd made up her mind. <...I am a not a good person. I've killed many people. I've deceived the innocent and the kind. And it wasn't for justice or a higher cause. It was all for myself, for my own satisfaction. But I have no regrets. Even now that I have seen this place for myself.>

Still sitting on the carpet, she looked up at the man seated on the stool.

The story she was about to tell...

...was, for her, a remorseless confession...

...and for him, an unbearable sin.

<Even if God were to give me the chance to turn back the hands of time, I would walk the same path.>

With that preface, the woman began her tale.

Chapter
1

On the island lived a silver dragon.

The place was a paradise for animals. Fragrant fruits grew in abundance.

The dragon dwelled in a fan-shaped cove. The area had originally been beautiful, with white-sand beaches as far as the eye could see.

But now the white sands were red, as if they'd been splattered with crimson paint. The ruins of a ship floated on the dark sea. The choking scent of iron mingled with the bloody tides.

Viscera and yellow fat drifted in the ocean of blood.

Just ten minutes ago, the mountain of gore had been living, breathing people.

This was what had become of those who'd attacked the island where the silver dragon lived. It had to be about twenty people, all told. And all of them had become piles of flesh. None moved—aside from the occasional posthumous spasm of a random corpse.

To the silver dragon, it was a familiar sight.

The dragon had received the order from God to protect all life on this island.

Since time immemorial, the silver dragon had fought off the island's attackers.

The humans had been attacking more often lately. Their weaponry had advanced remarkably, as well. The devices they called guns would be particularly troublesome if their technology progressed further. But still, he would not be killed for a while yet.

The blue-eyed silver dragon looked down at his body—at the scales that glowed faintly in the dim light and the dark-gray mercury-like fluid that flowed from the cracks between them.

This silvery liquid was the dragon's blood.

The humans had peppered the silver dragon with hundreds of bullets. One of these had gotten in between its dense scales and reached its flesh. Although, to the massive silver dragon, the sensation was akin to being pricked with a needle.

The shining silver droplets fell over a lump of meat.

No… Looking more closely, it wasn't a lump of meat at all.

The droplets had fallen on a child.

The child had to be only two or three years old. The dragon had no way of knowing its exact age. Its little body, splattered with blood, had looked like a savaged pile of meat. But its chest rose and fell gently.

The child was still alive.

But it would be dead soon. The silver dragon had doomed it.

The child wasn't covered in the same red blood of their surroundings, but the silver blood of the dragon.

A dragon's blood was potent and powerful. Humans had once used it as a reagent to cast mighty spells, but even then, a single drop had to be diluted many, many times. The untreated blood was practically a lethal venom. If a human was to touch it—let alone a child—they would almost certainly be killed.

The thunderous waves roared as if to snuff out the sound of the little life's heartbeat.

The dragon spread its enormous silver wings. He was preparing to return to the temple he called home.

Though he was a dragon, he wasn't heartless. But he had a far different view on life and death than a human would.

Weak creatures will die, while strong creatures will live. This is the way of the world God created.

That was one of the truths in the dragon's heart—and a lesson from the creator.

Whether they were a child or an adult, it mattered not in the face of God's teachings.

And so, the dragon flew off, leaving the defenseless child behind.

A short while later—perhaps it was a week, or maybe a month— the dragon returned to the cove once more. He had a craving for whale meat.

There was no longer a single body left in the cove. The corpses had been washed away by the white waves. The white sand sparkled like stardust.

The silver dragon dove into the ocean. While traveling underwater, he folded his wings in, adopting a streamlined form more appropriate for swimming.

In the deep ocean, about five hundred meters away from the island, he found a whale. He had been swimming for less than a minute. He hadn't thought he would be able to find something this quickly. A lucky find, indeed.

The dragon opened his jaw and snapped at the whale's torso. The whale was larger than the dragon, but the dragon was much faster—and much, much stronger.

Finally, the dragon took hold of the whale with his mouth and then rushed to the surface of the water. It happened too fast for the whale to process. Its mind still reeling, the whale lost consciousness. The change in pressure from the sudden rise to the surface had killed the whale before the dragon could even deal a mortal blow.

The dragon craned his neck like a whip and flung the whale toward shore.

The humongous creature scattered water droplets as it flew through the air in an arc. The seabirds that were lazily riding the air current scattered in a panic.

The corpse of the whale landed in the cove of the island the dragon lived, causing the ground to shake with the impact.

The dragon returned to the island and began to devour the whale's flesh.

Once he had filled his stomach with a third of the whale's meat, the dragon was satisfied. He would eat the rest another time.

Just as he was about to return to the temple once more, the dragon noticed a creature.

The creature loosely resembled a small monkey.

It was the dying human child. The dragon had completely forgotten about it.

The dragon's blue eyes widened.

It had been showered with dragon's blood...and survived.

He could see now that it was a girl child with black hair and black eyes. She wore a dress—child-size, but of good make. It was very wrinkled, as if she'd tried to wash the blood out with seawater. Try as she might, it seemed she had been unable to get the red stains out entirely.

The little child stood firmly on her two legs as she watched the dragon from behind a tree. She was wary of him. Although she did appear to be near starvation, she was very much alive.

The dragon quickly understood that this was the influence of its blood.

Dragon's blood was deadly.

If one sprayed ten thousand humans with it, nine thousand nine hundred and ninety-nine humans could be expected to die.

But one would survive. And if that one could withstand the potency of the blood and survive, then that human would be imbued with the power of the dragon itself.

This child had to be the exception—that one in ten thousand. Surely that was why she could stand on steady legs, even after being bathed in dragon's blood at an impossibly young age.

Ah, so that's how it is, the dragon thought.

Be it fate, heaven's decree, or the will of God, this youngling had managed to survive.

The dragon made a decision in that moment and started for the temple.

While flying through the sky, the dragon thought about how the child's skin had been unnaturally yellow and dry. He felt a pang of worry. He then looked down to see the little girl racing over to the whale carcass. She wasted no time stuffing her cheeks with as much whale meat as she could manage.

Within the day, the dragon returned to the cove. He had not come back to eat the rest of the whale.

When he approached the cove, he spotted the little girl right away. She was running toward the tree line to escape the dragon's shadow.

The dragon touched down on the shimmering sand. Once again, he noticed her watching him from behind a tree. No—more accurately, she was eyeing the whale carcass.

Surely, the child thought that the dragon had come back to finish his meal. The concern was plain on her face—she hoped from the pit of her empty stomach that there would be food left over. Her sunken eyes and yellowish skin were stark evidence of her poor nutrition. What had she been eating to survive? Insects? Tree roots?

<Come,> the dragon called out to the child.

She jumped.

<No need to be afraid. I'm not going to eat you. That you yet live is God's will.>

What the dragon had command of was not human language.

It was the True Language—words of power granted by God.

The language had been used long ago, before man had been divided into many tribes and had come to speak a variety of languages. With the True Language, it was possible to communicate with any living creature. The language was universal, making it possible to communicate what you wanted to say regardless of one's intellect or knowledge.

The dragon spoke to the child in a gentle tone, but she still seemed a bit apprehensive. That was no surprise. After all, the dragon was a full fifteen meters tall.

To indicate that he bore her no ill will, the silver dragon slowly craned his neck in a dramatic bow.

And then he offered a certain something he had hooked on one of his claws.

It was a bundle of fruits of every color. They had been growing around the temple he lived in.

The harvest had been a delicate operation for one so large, so a number of the fruits had been crushed when he had plucked them.

<Eat this fruit. Consuming only beast flesh and insects is not proper for a human diet. Though you have bathed in my blood and grown strong, you will still die at this rate.>

It took some time for the child to take that first step forward, but once she did, she was quick on her feet. She pattered up to the dragon, retrieved a fruit from his claw, and took a hearty bite.

<It's yummy,> the child said, and even she was surprised by what she'd just said. The little girl had suddenly become able to speak the True Language.

The fruit she had taken a bite of could be compared to the apples or pears familiar to humans. But it was much more than a simple fruit.

<You have tasted the fruit of knowledge. It grants wisdom and intelligence to those who consume it.>

Thanks to the intellect granted by the fruit, and the universality of the True Language, the child had become able to communicate without any difficulty.

The child covered her small mouth with both hands.

<Oh no! I heard in an old story that it's a sin for humans to eat the fruit of knowledge...>

<Ha-ha, not quite. It is not a sin to eat the fruit of knowledge. The sin lies in using the knowledge granted by the fruit for treachery, such as deceiving and tricking another. You may eat without fear.>

Relieved to hear that, the child brought the rest of the fruit to her mouth. Watching this charming sight, the dragon warned the child, <Through the fruit of knowledge, you will now be more sensitive than others to the subtleties of the human heart. You must not use this gift to deceive others. Remember, God is watching you.>

The child nodded as she continued to eat.

After devouring the fruit, the child said, <Thank you.>

Her unnaturally yellowish and dry skin regained its vibrancy. Even in terms of nutritional value, the fruit of knowledge was clearly different from the fruit of the lands of men.

<Why did you save me?>

<It was not I who saved you, but God. God saved your life.>

<God?>

<You survived, even after being bathed in my blood. I have interpreted that as the will of God—that you are not to die yet.>

<Does God really exist?>

<He does. This island has actually been blessed by God.>

The fruit of knowledge grew here, as did the tree of life, and nectar flowed along its streams. This island was just such a place.

<Where am I?> asked the girl.

<A remote island in the middle of the ocean. I've heard humans call it the Island of Silver, but the name God gave it was Eden.>

Then the dragon asked, <You came here without knowing what this place is?>

The little child nodded. <I was taken away by some scary people, and before I knew it, I was here.>

Taken away.

Making note of the child's otherwise ornate dress, the silver dragon thought for a moment.

The dragon was not at all versed in worldly affairs, but he did understand that the clothes she wore were those of an aristocrat. It was said that some despicable humans would pillage and kidnap—so this child had to be a victim.

<I will take you to the lands of men,> the dragon proposed.

But the child said, <I don't want to go,> hanging her head.

<Don't you have a family waiting for you?>

The silver dragon had killed many humans. They had all been after his blood or the island's treasure—or else posed some other threat. But that did not change the fact that he had taken many lives.

He had primarily slain adult men. On the verge of death, even the burliest men would cry for their mothers more often than not. They would wail their throats raw. They would cry for figures who could do little to affect the outcome, even if they had been present.

Thus, the child's remarks were unexpected.

<You do have parents, don't you?>

<I do, but…I don't know their faces.>

The child was expressionless.

<A home tutor cared for me. She said my parents were nobles, so I had to become a proper lady. It was like that for all my elder siblings, too. My brother might have gotten some attention

from my father, though. But to me, it was like not having parents
at all.>

The child looked at the dragon with her big eyes.

<What about you?> she asked. <Are you all alone here, too?>

<No,> the dragon said. <Lend me your ear. Now that you can speak
the True Language, you should be able to understand...the mean-
ings of the cries of the forest animals, and the insects' buzzing, and the
birds' chirping.>

The True Language enabled communication with all living creatures.

Now the child understood the animals that lived in peace in the forest,
and she understood that they were sincerely happy.

<That's so nice...> In a yearning tone, the child said, <I'd like to stay
here, too.>

<If that is what you wish, then you should.>

The child opened her round eyes wide and looked at the dragon.
<Really? It's really okay?>

<Of course. However, if you're going to live here in Eden, then
you must folllow God's teachings.>

<God's teachings?>

<No creature here in Eden may fight. You must not harbor hate,
resentment, or loathing in your heart. Here, we are all family. We
have love and affection for one another. If you can promise that,
then you can stay here, too.>

<That's easy. If that's the rule here, then the creatures of Eden
won't bully me, right? I'd never hate or loathe them. I'll keep that
promise.>

<All right. Then that makes you and me family.>

The child smiled innocently. <Hey, what should I call you? My name
is—>

<That won't be necessary. Since this is not the lands of men, I
will call you *you*. And you will also call me *you*. As long as we have
love for each other, names will not be necessary.>

<Okay?>

<And no more of that girlish lilt. Overt differences in the

sexes can give rise to discrimination. You should speak in a plain manner.>

<A plain manner? ...What do you mean?> The child added, <Oh, maybe I should just, um, imitate you,> changing her manner of speech.

The dragon lifted the child onto his back and flew to the temple where he lived.

The child quickly became friends with the animals. It was fortunate that she was only three years old. If she had been a little older, with her heart sullied by the world, then she probably wouldn't have been able to establish a bond with the residents of Eden.

The child loved the flowers, sang to the wind, and raced through the fields with the rabbits.

She grew close with many different animals, but the one she became especially attached to was the dragon.

<He was the first to show me kindness.>

When she slept, she always leaned against the dragon's tail, torso, or neck.

The dragon considered that perhaps the child thought of him as her parent—a father who shared her blood.

The child grew incredibly quickly.

The dragon's blood and the fruit of knowledge had transformed her into a creature overflowing with vitality.

Nine years passed, and the toddler grew into a young girl.

If she had been an average human, then she would still have been around eleven or twelve, but the brilliance of her intellect was comparable to an adult's, and her physical growth surpassed a human twelve-year-old's. The blessings from the fruit of God had accelerated her body's growth, so she became quite tall for her age, and her chest swelled. Sometimes, she could be seen being embarrassed by courtship attempts from brilliantly colored birds, resplendent peacocks, and mighty eagles.

The girl ran faster than the horses living on the island, was stronger than a boar, and became nimbler than a snake.

But over the course of her growth, it was her overall change in color that stood out more than anything. The color of her hair had changed from jet-black…to silver.

It was due to the mercury-like dragon's blood that had rained over her. The girl's hair was now the same color as the dragon's scales.

Her skin became snow-white, her eyes red as if filled with blood, and her hair silver like the moon. All pigment had seeped out of her.

It was around this time that humans targeting Eden visited its shores once more.

The dragon responded to the humans' invasion, heading out to the cove to drive off their boat—just as he always had.

But in a mere nine years, human technology had progressed by leaps and bounds.

Their handheld firearms were not yet powerful enough to defeat the dragon. But the military vessel that came to attack was equipped with dozens of cannons with enough power to pierce a dragon's scales. Though the submachine guns the humans carried were, as before, not much different from peashooters, fired from a suitable distance, they could crack his scales, at least.

The sounds of bombardment rang out intermittently. The sparks lit the nighttime sea red.

Silver blood scattered. It was a light wound, but it would look to another like a dramatic spray.

While breaking the warship in two, the dragon thought.

…*This won't last much longer.*

His thoughts weren't on the enemy then… He was thinking about his own longevity.

Judging from the remarkably swift development of military tech, in another ten years—no, perhaps even five, human technology would reach the point where their machinations could deal him a fatal blow. Yes, he was coolly analyzing it.

But he didn't mind.

The strong would live, and the weak would die. This was the way of the world God created.

The dragon's era was coming to an end. That was all.

I am not long for this world.

He suddenly noticed that the irritating spray of submachine gun fire had ceased.

The dragon had not dealt with those attackers. He was preoccupied with the warship.

Yet at some point, the humans who had landed on the beach had all died.

No… They had been killed.

The cove was red with blood—a sight similar to the scene he was responsible for nine years prior.

At the center of the carnage, there stood a little dragon.

Her long silver hair, left to grow as it pleased, trailed in the wind. Her white clothes were like flapping wings.

The girl danced around the battlefield, effortlessly evading the storm of bullets as she took life after life. She struck one man with a supple leg, and his head burst open. Her dainty palm pierced straight through another enemy's chest, armor and all.

She was every bit the daughter of the silver dragon. It was as if a little dragon were helping her parent.

Yet…no.

Surely the girl wanted to believe it was so.

That she was the silver dragon's daughter.

The dragon felt a pang of sadness in his chest.

Having fended off the humans, the dragon and the girl returned to the temple. The girl was worried about the dragon's wound, but she was relieved to learn it was minor. Fortunately, she had not sustained any injuries.

<What do we do?> the girl asked, gritting her teeth. <The human weapons are developing so quickly. At this rate…you'll be killed. You're Eden's protector.>

<Indeed. In the near future, I will be killed,> the dragon replied.

<Why do the humans keep coming to this island?>

<Because Eden has many of God's creations…such as the tree of life and the fruit of knowledge. Humans lust after those things because happiness in this life is their greatest conundrum—their ever-fleeting quarry.>

<But if you die, all those things will be turned to ash.>

The silver dragon was the guardian of Eden.

When the guardian died, Eden would burn. The fruit of knowledge, the tree of life, and the nectar—all of it would become ash. God would not hand His creations over to the unworthy.

<Even as ash, the creations of Eden can be used as valuable resources. As the Guardian of Eden, I am an exception—when I die, my body will not become ash.>

The dragon's fat would be made into potent fuel, its blood would be processed into powerful medicine, its scales armor, its teeth swords, its flesh nutrients—all priceless treasures.

To the humans, Eden and the dragon that protected it were worth pursuing, no matter the sacrifice.

<But we…just want to live in peace…without causing trouble for anyone…,> the girl said.

The dragon's blue eyes beheld the troubled girl. <Do you want to live?>

The girl tilted her head and said, <Isn't that obvious?>

It was not obvious.

In the lands of men, attachment to life could be taken for granted. But this island was different. After the creatures of Eden died, their souls were guaranteed salvation. Therefore, although creatures born in Eden did not seek death, neither did they mourn it.

Could it be…? This child…

Telling her to wait for a while, the dragon headed to the depths of the temple.

Long, long ago, there had been a time when the silver dragon was revered by humans. Whenever people were struck with natural disaster, or when other nations went to war with them, the people would bequeath offerings to the dragon. Gems, gold and silver, flowers, clothing, dolls, grains, young women.

I had no use for any of those things…

But perhaps the child would need them.

The room where the dragon arrived contained many offerings.

The dragon stood there before gems of many colors. He knew that human women liked gemstones. But a dragon could not understand human tastes. Which of these dazzlingly shining stones should he choose?

He considered the options for a while, but it soon became clear that this was a fruitless endeavor, no matter how much time he spent deliberating. So the dragon chose a treasure, taking the greatest care not to nick it as he made his way back to the girl.

Laid atop his great claws was a garnet necklace. He had chosen it because it was the same color as the girl's eyes. <I want you to have this.>

The girl accepted the garnet. <This is...for me?> *How pretty*, she said in a delighted tone, then hugged the gem to her chest. <I'm so happy. Just as happy as that time you gave me the fruit.>

Then the dragon was certain. <If you like it, then I'm glad.>

He was glad, but sad.

A creature of Eden would not have been pleased by a gem.

This child belonged in the lands of men, after all.

The dragon pointed with a claw to the room where the offerings were kept. <There are even more gems in that room. There are clothes, too. All of it is yours. You should dress yourself however you like.>

Still clasping the garnet, the girl nodded, then went into the offerings room.

With sad eyes, the dragon watched her go innocently.

The girl stayed alone in that room for nearly two hours.

The dragon continued to wait for her. The dragon would not grow angry and impatient as a human would, no matter how long he was kept waiting. Having lived thousands of years, two hours was equivalent to the blink of an eye.

When the girl emerged from the room, she was dressed in deep red from head to toe—dress, corset, blouse, and ribbon.

All of it was the same color as the garnet.

<There should have been clothing of many different colors in that room,> said the dragon.

‹I like red.› The girl had proudly declared it was her new favorite color.

‹...Away from this island,› the dragon continued, ‹there is even more clothing—and more gems as well. There will be lots of the things you like—and many more red things.›

The girl gave the dragon a startled look. Red eyes and blue eyes met.

‹No...,› said the girl. It seemed she didn't want the dragon to continue. ‹What I want can only be found on this island.›

‹Hear me.›

The girl shook her head, but the dragon ignored her and continued. ‹Once I die, the things of this island will turn to ash. But only the things of this island. You are not of this island. You were born away from here. When I die, you will not become ash. Even after I die, you must continue to live—away from this island.›

Upon speaking plainly, the dragon suddenly realized—

It seemed he did not want the girl to die.

‹There's no place for me away from this island,› said the girl.

‹You've only ever spent two or three years away from this island, haven't you? You simply had bad fortune for those two or three years. Surely there are humans who will be kind to you.›

The girl shook her head fiercely. Droplets scattered from the corners of her eyes to splatter on the marble floor.

‹Even still,› the girl went on. ‹Still... You're the very first one who was ever kind to me.›

‹It was you, and no one else,› the girl said with tears building again. ‹I want to be with you.›

The dragon felt the same.

All the creatures of Eden were family, but the girl was special to him. He figured that had to be because he'd been watching over the girl since she was a small child. Not having a bond of blood, he couldn't be certain, but...

It seems that I've come to love this girl as a father.

The girl said, ‹I don't want you to die. All the creatures of Eden are family...but you're special to me.›

She said exactly what the dragon had been thinking.

<The next time the humans attack, let's flee the island together,> the girl continued. <One of a dragon's secret abilities is to assume the form of a human, right? Let's disguise ourselves as humans and survive together.>

That was a request he could not grant.

<God has entrusted me with the task to protect Eden. I cannot abandon it.>

But still.

<Does God really exist?> the girl asked. <If He is real, then why doesn't He help us? We haven't done anything wrong.>

<God will save us. Now you listen to me. What I'm about to say, you must not ever forget. In Eden, we have lived without hating or loathing anyone, with love and respect for one another. This manner of benevolence is impossible in the lands of men.>

So God does exist.
If you've done good things, then you will know salvation.

<When a soul has accumulated good deeds,> the dragon went on, <it will be taken to the Kingdom of Eternity after death. There lies paradise eternal. There, you shall live forever, without being stricken by illness or withered by age, and can spend everlasting life with the ones you love. Of course, there is also no fear of threats from the sea. I want to see you in the Kingdom of Eternity. So even after you have ventured to the lands of men, you must not doubt God. You must not turn your back on these teachings.>

<So in other words, God says, *I'll save your soul, so for now, give up and die?*>

It was then that the dragon realized the three years before the girl had come to this island had been fatal.

He had thought back then that, since she'd been a small child, it was not yet too late.

But this girl did not believe in God. Therefore, she could not accept that the structure of the world was so sincerely open, concealing nothing.

In the most fundamental areas, my daughter is a human still.

<...I understand. Let us go to the lands of men together. Let us try living in the human world a little,> the dragon said, but this was not because he had decided that he would live with the girl as a human.

It was in order to get her used to the human world... To the place she had to return.

It took three days for the dragon's wounds to fully heal.

On the night they were to leave for the lands of men, the dragon gave her one of his scales. <Swallow this. If you do, then you'll be able to transform into a full-fledged dragon for a short while.>

The girl swallowed the scale without a second thought. Her small body began to change, and in the blink of an eye, she had become a little dragon.

When they stood side by side, the big dragon and the little dragon really did look like parent and child.

The two dragons left the island for the lands of men.

They were headed for the capital of an empire called Norvelland. It was the most glorious city in the empire, Nibelungen.

But clearly they couldn't land directly in Nibelungen. The silver dragons' wings would stand out far too much. First, the dragons headed to a deserted location a short distance from the city.

Fortunately for them, no one saw them land.

The large dragon used a secret art to transform into a young man. The color of his short hair was the same silver as his scales.

The little dragon returned to her humanoid form. She simply had to wish to return to human form to make it so.

The two humans were naked.

The girl hid her chest and privates with her hands and sat down.

And then, with her face red as an apple, she said, <D-don't look...>

The man didn't understand why the girl would say such a thing, but he decided to turn his back to her.

He was the protective father who had raised the girl, and there was no doubt that the girl thought of him as her father as well. Being parent and child, there was nothing to be embarrassed about, even if they were both naked.

The man walked behind a nearby boulder. There, he had hidden a large bag. Inside was a set of the items needed for traveling, including clothes. He had brought them over during the day.

While ensuring that he didn't look at the girl, the man handed over some clothes for her. Behind him, he could hear her hastily clothing herself. Meanwhile, the man also dressed.

<You can look now…,> the girl said.

Standing there was a girl wearing the attire of a middle-class resident of the Norvelland Empire.

Properly clothed, the girl seemed to feel relieved, but now it was the man's turn to become nervous.

While transformed into a human, the dragon couldn't wield even 10 percent of his original power. It was possible that he was even weaker than the girl in this form. What's more, he'd heard that certain humans had eyes that could detect dragons in disguise. In the unlikely event that they were attacked, it would be difficult to protect the girl.

The sights of the countryside surrounded them. Off in the distance, the mountains were shrouded in darkness.

They made their way to a small stone bridge. This was the path that led to the capital.

The man took the girl's hand. <Stay by my side.> On the off chance that they were attacked, the man meant to protect the girl, even at the cost of his life.

The girl's cheeks were red. But this was nothing like a flush of embarrassment. She not only gave him her hand, but she even leaned into him.

Side by side, they walked through the night until they finally reached the city. Normal people would have felt terribly sore, but it was no problem for them.

They were before the main way in Nibelungen, under an arch where the name of the city was carved. Having finally reached the city, the silver man came to a stop.

He looked straight at the girl and said, <We are about to enter a human

city. And so, now I have a request of you.> His voice was tense. <I want you to avoid any preconceived notions as you look around. There will surely be kind people. There will surely be things you will enjoy.>

The girl nodded without thinking about it deeply.

The man didn't notice that her nod was not entirely honest.

Because the girl had already found something she enjoyed.

Just walking along the night road where there was nothing but country fields, pulled by the young man's had, the girl had been enjoying herself. Her heart was pounding. She wanted him to take her hand again, and this time, for him to draw her close.

She didn't tell him that she was already enjoying herself. She was worried that if she voiced it, their goal here would be done, and it would be over.

She wanted to keep walking with him.

The pair decided to stay at an inn that was neither expensive nor cheap, but right in the middle.

Leaving their bag in the room, they rested only a little before the two of them headed into the city.

Being that it was the capital, the city was bustling, indeed, and full of vitality.

But that was all.

There wasn't a single thing about this city the girl could enjoy.

She never felt any of the simple joys or pounding of her heart that she'd felt when they'd been walking together with the fields around them.

And that was because no matter where you looked…

…the city was overflowing with dragonslayers.

There were opera performances. The story depicted a hero killing the evil dragon Fafnir—or the story of God raining lightning down upon the treacherous dragon Lucifer and thrusting him down into hell. The singers loudly belted out their songs of the honor of heroes and humiliation of dragons.

There was a bronze statue in the square. It depicted a soldier thrusting a spear into a dragon's breast. The children running around the square were playing pretend and slaying dragons with make-believe weapons. The role of the dragonslayer was popular, and they all fought over it. In the end, a child who looked like the son of a soldier got the role of dragonslayer, and a timid-looking child had the role of evil dragon foisted on them.

There was a book being sold. It was an award-winning romance novel popular with women. The summary revealed that it was about a prince killing a dragon to save a princess, who he later wed.

The grilled meat of a small dragon was being sold at a food stall. They said that dragon fat was used as fuel for the fire that cooked the meat. The girl thought it was a nasty joke.

The disguised silver dragon had said there were surely kind people in this city, there would surely be things she enjoyed...

But to the girl...

...this bustling and resplendent city of Nibelungen...

...was nothing more than a nightmare made real.

Yet the girl walked on.

And that was because before passing through the arches, the young man had told her: <I want you to avoid any preconceived notions as you look around.>

On their third circle around, they found a group talking about the salvation of dragons. That was the only moment that the girl's heart leaped. But learning of the group's deeds caused her heart to sink again. That group was preaching that, when killing a dragon, it was necessary to give them a gentle death. They'd never had any intention of saving dragons' lives.

After three days, she'd had enough.

The dinner that was prepared for them at the inn tasted like sand in her mouth. The ingredients of the lands of men were far inferior to what could be harvested in Eden.

I wish we could have kept walking down the road that night forever.

The girl used a knife and fork to cut up her roast bird. She was intellectually aware of how to use utensils, but that didn't mean she was used to it. Her handling was a bit awkward.

Seeing that, the young man said, <You use the knife like this. Look.>

The young man sliced up the bird—beautifully and skillfully.

The girl's utensils clattered to the plate.

Enough was enough.

Instead of taking up her utensils, she could only clench her fists. They even trembled a little.

She couldn't take it anymore—not the opera, the statue, the children, the book, or the stores.

But more than that, she couldn't stand how her companion was so calm through it all.

<Do you feel *nothing*?> she demanded.

<What do you mean?> The young man brought a bite of meat to his mouth.

<Dragons are being killed, and their murders are being glorified. Their *flesh* is being *eaten*. Their fat made into fuel. Do you feel nothing even though you're a dragon, too?>

Since they were both speaking in the True Language, the other customers in the restaurant couldn't hear what they were saying.

<You must not let the fires of hatred burn within you. Remember, even if we meet an untimely end in this life, so long as our hearts are pure, we will meet again in the Kingdom of Eternity.>

The man swallowed. <The teachings of God dictate that we must hold no hatred for anyone.>

The girl bit her lip. <You feel no pain in your chest?>

<None.>

<Doesn't your head grow hot? You don't feel as though nothing matters? …Nothing, save the white-hot desire to thrust a knife into their flesh?> Her lip began to bleed. <You don't want to see this city burn?>

<You're bleeding. Stop biting your lip.>

<They won't mourn your death, you know…>

<There is no need for sadness. In fact, death is something to be glad for. After death, the Kingdom of Eternity awaits.>

In the end, humans were humans, and dragons were dragons.

Though they would never see eye to eye…

…they both carried the same feeling in their heart:

Why can't you understand something so simple?

On the fourth day, they went to a history museum.

The goal was to learn about the history of dragonslayers. It was the one thing the girl truly wanted. She had stopped showing interest in just about every other place in the city, but this one was different.

If there was any hope…

Heat raced around the girl's body. Her heart pounded in her chest.

…it could only be found in combat.

The blood of the dragon flowed in her veins. There was nothing to do but to use her inhuman power to take command of humans, just as in the old legends—from a time when dragons ruled the world.

Displayed in the history museum were tools and weapons that had been used to slay dragons. She was also able to get an understanding of the functionality of the latest weaponry. She observed this information with bloodshot eyes, drilling it into her head, and understood it.

"Ha-ha…" A laugh slipped from the girl's lips. "Ha…ha-ha…"

She covered her mouth. The visitors going back and forth eyed her with suspicion.

Let them think what they want. How could I not laugh?

It was absurd.

"To think that human science has developed so much…"

The naval fleet that had attacked the dragon's island had been no more than a diversion. It had served as reconnaissance, to see how powerful the dragon was—and as a way to dispose of a ship that was no longer in production.

The people who had been sent to attack Eden had not been regular, trained soldiers. They'd been death-row inmates and exiled criminals given weapons.

A movie projector played in black-and-white on the museum screen.

A dragon even larger than the silver dragon was engaged in combat with humans.

No…not humans, but a machine.

A vehicle made of iron. It was equipped with a large gun barrel.

It was apparently called a heavily armored tank.

The gun barrel on top of the tank aimed at the dragon.

The Balmung Cannon. That was the name of the armament.

The black-and-white footage had no audio.

For an instant, the screen went all white, and then a moment later, there was a great hole in the chest of the giant dragon.

When the giant dragon fell, the footage shuddered violently. There was a boom as a curtain of dust was swept up.

How could they hope to fight something like *that*?

The power of a dragon was so outdated.

<Live with me, in human form. In some faraway village,> the girl said to the young man when they left the museum.

<I can't do that. Please, try to understand.>

I can't understand, the girl said. <So what about God? I don't care about Him, or demons, or angels. I…> After a pause, the girl eventually steeled herself and opened her mouth again. <I love you.>

The man nodded as well. <I love you, too.>

That's not what I mean, the girl said. <I love you as a father… But in another sense, as well…>

The man's eyes opened wide, and he covered his face with a hand. <…Oh, what a disaster. Even in Eden, this is not allowed.>

<Because I'm human…and you're a dragon?>

<You understand that's not the reason, don't you?>

There was no problem with a union between human and dragon. Since Eden was a place of freedom, even a human and wolf could be united.

The problem was that their relationship was that of parent and child. Even if they were not related by blood, romantic feelings between parent and child were one of the few taboos that existed in Eden.

Even the girl had to know of that taboo. But the words that flowed out of her could not be stopped. <It's because I love you that I want you to live.>

The man's faith kept him from answering.

<I see,> the girl muttered. <You're content with dying, no matter what?> she asked the dragon.

<...Yes.>

<Then I will die with you.>

<But...>

<Being in this city has taught me something. Dragons have no allies anywhere in the world.>

So I will be the only one.

<I will be the only one to remain by your side, until the very end.>

Looking at the girl's face, the man was surprised.

The anger that had just been burning with in her, the ugly hate, the forbidden love—it was all gone.

Humans might call that look understanding—or perhaps resignation. The dragon could not tell the difference.

<I'll go with you to the Kingdom of Eternity,> the girl said. <There...will I be allowed to love you?>

<Yes... If it's in the Kingdom of Eternity, then surely...>

No rules or taboos existed in the Kingdom of Eternity. It was a place of true freedom.

When they left the lands of men, it was as if an evil spirit left the girl as well.

As she was now, God would surely save her.

With this belief in his heart, the dragon returned with the girl to the island, deciding they would welcome the destruction that would one day visit—together.

The island was peaceful for a time.

In the unchanging paradise of animals, abundant fruit grew, and the temple was magnificent and beautiful.

Perhaps the four days they had spent in the lands of men had just been a bad dream. There couldn't be any place in the world that was truly so horrible. Since returning to the island, they knew nothing but peace.

Four years passed, and the girl turned sixteen.

Showered by the blood of the dragon and eating the fruit of knowledge that grew from the tree of life, plus having continuously slaked her thirst on nectar, she possessed near-perfect physical beauty. Her visage was incredibly close to that of the very first woman, created by God.

Her heart was open, her expressions abundant.

Every night, the girl sang songs of love to the dragon.

Her voice was so sweet that it just about melted the dragon's mind away. At times, he felt that he might yield himself to her.

I like you.

The dragon replied that he liked her, too.

I love you.

The dragon replied that he loved her, too.

The dragon's resolve remained firm. He made sure things never progressed any further.

It was because he loved the girl. So long as they committed no taboo and lived righteously, they would be united when they met in the Kingdom of Eternity.

Thinking of the destruction that would visit soon, nothing would be more foolish than to reciprocate the girl's true feelings. To abandon their eternal lives in a paradise in exchange for a few years of pleasure…

The day of destruction came without warning.

The dragon was asleep in the temple. The girl wore a crimson dress and cuddled up next to him, singing a song of love in his ear.

The sonorous melody stopped abruptly.

The girl had noticed something strange.

First came the stench. It was a faint smell that only the girl noticed.

Next, the sound.

A sound like bee's buzzing lightly struck her ears. Next, there came the sound of something crumbling. She could hear it from the other side of the white dome.

Suddenly, there was a roar, and the temple shuddered. The dragon's eyes opened, and he raised his head.

The girl and dragon left the temple.

The girl had thought that when their last day on the island finally came, she would be fighting a tank.

But what she and the dragon faced was none other than a fighter aircraft. There were countless hunks of metal flying through the night sky.

The attack was an air raid.

The dragon beat the air with his wings. Stirring up a violent wind, he leaped into the sky.

With his fangs, claws, and the fire from his mouth, he fought the fighter aircraft.

Having no wings, there was nothing at all the girl could do to help.

The silver dragon was strong.

He brought down one, two, three fighter aircraft.

It was no wonder the girl's heart was racing so hard.

Since his bravery, his boldness, and his great size were symbols of invincibility to her.

Since even knowing how high performance human weapons were, the girl had never seen the silver dragon lose even once.

The fighter aircraft fled.

The dragon pursued them.

The girl followed the dragon as he headed to the cove. All she could do was watch and wait.

…At first, she thought she was mistaken.

Even though there was no way he could be wounded, it looked as if the dragon was flying lower.

When she reached the cove, she became certain.

The power was gone from his wingbeats, and he was losing altitude before her eyes. The girl couldn't tell what was happening. The dragon's breaths had grown ragged, like he was in pain.

The girl and dragon had assumed the first attack had been an aerial strike. But that was not the case.

Prior to the bombing, many smoking, bomb-like objects had been dropped around the temple. They hadn't exploded, but had quietly harmed the dragon in a different way, eating into him.

The girl realized what that faint stench really was.

The first weapon used against the dragon had been poison gas.

Victory had been decided before the fight had even begun, since even the fighter planes the dragon had taken down had been a decoy for luring the dragon out to the cove.

It was a compound that only worked on dragons. Before her eyes, the nerves of his body were paralyzed. As the dragon reached the cove, he landed on the beach, audibly skidding through the sand.

The dragon's blue eyes gazed at the ocean and the enemies there.

The fleet floated on the water, about twenty kilometers ahead. Surrounded by little gunships that were like hangers-on, an abnormally imposing battleship pointed its main gun at the dragon.

The girl had seen that gun before.

The girl realized…

The four days she'd spent in the lands of men had been no nightmare.

In fact, the days she had spent on this island might well have been no more than a sweet dream.

The Balmung Cannon.

Its gun barrel aimed at where the dragon lay on the ground.

The girl ran to the dragon.

She didn't know whether she could be useful, but she raced over anyway.

Her left arm reached out to the dragon.

At the same time, a flash of light tore through the darkness of night.

In the next moment, her body was hurtling through the air. The blast of light eviscerated everything from the girl's chest to her right arm.

It was incredibly powerful.

Even if she had managed to fully position herself between the dragon and the cannon, it wouldn't have made a difference.

Her body slammed to the beach with a grisly splat. She didn't die immediately, thanks to the dragon's blood. But she could no longer move.

The girl struggled to adjust her head enough to look at the dragon.

The dragon was wounded just as badly—no, he was in much worse condition than the girl.

The right side of his body was gone. The scales that should have been solid had melted like candy, and pieces of his shredded right wing had fallen to the beach.

Mercury-like blood had started to flow like a waterfall.

The silver dragon was dead.

There was no life in his blue eyes.

The plants behind him were burning.

With the dragon's death, the whole island was enveloped in flames in an instant.

Seeing that, the girl felt like black sparks were crackling deep in her body.

This is strange.

The girl had imagined this tragedy in her mind many times. Every time, she had steeled herself. She understood that they would be united in the Kingdom of Eternity, so she should have welcomed death.

But even understanding that…

The girl could see tears in the dragon's eyes.

No, dragons were not made to cry tears. Blood was flowing from his eyes, which had been damaged in the blast. It only appeared as though he were crying.

But seeing him like this…

The girl moved her neck. She looked at the battleship that had dealt the mortal blow to the dragon.

Standing by the battery was a man who looked like he had fired the gun. It was far enough away that a normal human wouldn't be able to see, but having been bathed in the dragon's blood, the girl could clearly see his face.

He was a soldier with black hair and dot-like irises. Though he stared at the girl and the dragon, he appeared to feel nothing…or so she thought at first. But the man's nasty-looking eyes were on the burning Eden.

The man's mouth moved. Having been showered with the dragon's blood, the girl could hear what he was saying, even across the great distance.

"…Come on, not again… Why do dragons…never know when to give up? Putting up a pathetic struggle to the last. We just want the fruit…"

The man clicked his tongue, saying, "Another waste."

With a whoosh, the sparks within the girl roared into full bloom.

A waste?

Did that man just say it was a waste?

After disturbing our peace, burning our paradise, and stealing away the lives of those we loved…

…He calls that a waste?

With all sorts of negative emotions—sorrow, regret, hatred, and rage—as kindling, a fire blazed to life in her heart.

I cannot die.

The girl's body was wet with the dragon's blood that overflowed from the corpse beside her.

They will not have it.

Since they have the nerve to consider this a waste.

The girl sucked up the silver blood that soaked the beach. Refusing to hand over even a drop, she fervently dragged her tongue over the sand to lick it up and swallow.

She had to survive. She figured that if she consumed the dragon's blood, she might be able to do something about her fatal wounds.

If I can kill that man…

The fires of vengeance burned in the girl's red eyes.

If I can kill that man, I don't need anything else.

The girl continued to voraciously lap up the bodily fluids of the one she loved, but no matter how frantic she became, she couldn't stop her vision from growing dark.

Eventually, her consciousness faded to black.

In the end, human and dragon could not understand one another, to the last.

The amphibious assault ship *Fredegund*.

It was the name of the battleship that had killed the silver dragon, with five escort ships in tow.

The captain was Sigebert Siegfried. He was a naval officer of the Norvelland Empire.

Sigebert was the head of the Siegfried family, a clan famous for being dragonslayers. But he didn't look much like a dragonslaying hero. He was tall but too skinny, with a constant nasty look in his dot-like eyes. His voice was low and quiet—and oddly viscous. On top of that, he spoke very slowly. A ruby pendant hung from his neck.

Sigebert was watching the blazing island with a fed-up expression.

Another Eden's gone and burned up…

The islands that the dragons protected were all called Edens. They dotted the world, and all of them were overflowing with resources unknown to humans—such as the fruit of knowledge that appeared in legend—or so it was said.

So it was *said*, because no one had ever actually acquired these fruits of knowledge.

Whenever a landing operation had been attempted…or rather, when a dragon was killed, the island it inhabited went up in flames. But then occupying the island without killing the dragon was very difficult. Once before, a dragon had been taken alive, at great cost—but the moment it had been captured, the island burned all the same.

As a result, all that could be acquired were the cinders, which came to be known as the Ashes of Eden. But this was also fairly valuable as a resource. Even as ash, creations of Eden were very powerful.

Now Edens all over the world were turning to ash.

Normally, one should be searching for a way to occupy the Edens without setting the islands ablaze, but there were reasons that wasn't possible. Since the product known as the Ashes of Eden was very energy dense, all the nations on Earth were looking to acquire it.

The Norvelland Imperial Army, in which Commodore Sigebert served, held an advantage over other nations in the conquest of Edens, but at the same time, they absolutely couldn't afford to fall behind.

They were at an advantage over other nations because they had Commodore Sigebert—that is to say, the dragonslayer Siegfried. The progress in modern weaponry was remarkable, but it was still difficult to kill a dragon. So that was where a dragonslayer was needed. The Balmung Cannon, which only Sigebert Siegfried could control, would kill any dragon in one hit. The technique could only be executed by one of the Siegfried blood, and no other nation could emulate it.

The reason they couldn't afford to fall behind was because the Norvelland Empire was lacking in its own resources. The Norvelland Empire was one of the great powers on the continent of Europa, but a major part of that was that they had managed to monopolize the resources of Eden through their ability to kill dragons. There were still not many examples of other nations succeeding in occupying an Eden, but there would certainly be more to come. And so, they had decided that they didn't care if it was just ash—they would forestall other nations to retrieve all the resources from every remaining Eden.

The soldiers took the landing boats to Eden, doing their best to put out the fires, but well, it would be ash this time, too. The researchers had said that "We don't understand the logic, but the fruits of Eden burn from the inside out." It was as if God was refusing to deliver them into the hands of humanity.

Eventually, one of the landing vessels returned. Sigebert didn't concern himself with it, figuring it was just the vanguard back with some ash.

But before long, Sigebert's good friend raced up to him in a panic.

"Oh, God! Sigebert! They found something incredible!"

It was a man called Johann Sachs. He was quite flustered, but he did, in fact, have the rank of colonel. Sigebert outranked him, but the two had a friendship that went beyond that. Still, when they were in the field, the man should have been treating his superior officer with respect. His subordinates were watching, after all.

"Calm down. You're turning forty this year," said Sigebert.

"You're the same age as me! Agh, good God! Just come out here already! Hurry! She might die! Then you'll definitely regret it!"

With Colonel Sachs dragging him along, Commodore Sigebert headed to where the landing vessels were kept.

The girl was unconscious on her back on the iron floor. Her silver hair had a bewitching luster to it. She was a mature-looking girl. She was wearing a red dress, but her right arm had been blown off, and she was still bleeding.

"…What about her? This is the woman who just about died defending the dragon. I saw her, too."

The Siegfried clan had superhuman abilities, perhaps because of their heroic blood. He had fired on the dragon from over ten miles away, but he had been able to clearly see what had happened there.

It was rare to find people living on Edens. But they would always die with the dragons or burn up like the fruit did. The researchers divided them into two camps. There were those who washed ashore on an Eden and would ultimately take their own lives once the dragons perished. Then there were those who were born on an Eden and would naturally catch fire once the island began to burn. Sigebert wasn't sure how the researchers arrived at these two classifications of humans discovered on Edens.

This girl seemed to be of the former.

"Let her die with it."

Even without him saying that, this girl was going to die anyway. It was one thing to lose an arm, but the blast had also taken a large chunk out of the right side of her chest. Her right lung was gone—there was no way she was going to survive.

"You idiot! Look at her left wrist!" Sachs yelled.

"…Hm?"

Tattooed on her thin wrist was the crest of a certain noble family.

The silver dragon…

The one I loved was right in front of me.

I rushed up to him and embraced him. The scales that should have been hard were soft like a rotten fruit. The harder I squeezed, the farther my arms sank into his flesh.

Something sticky came to fall on top of my head.

The dragon's body was melting, becoming liquid. The dragon's head, which had half liquefied, had fallen into my hair. His bodily fluids dripped from the ends of my bangs, and I licked them away with my tongue.

I buried my face in his stomach.

Like nibbling, like eating, like biting, like slurping, like drinking, like licking—

—like kissing…

I am taken into him. I take him in.

It didn't feel so bad. No, I'll say it clearly. It actually filled me with euphoria.
Violating the will of the one I loved to become one with him…
…felt so comfortable it defied imagination…
…and so good it frightened me.

With the sensation of a blanket touching her fingertips, the girl's eyes opened.

She was in bed in the infirmary of a Norvelland Imperial Army camp.

Her vision was hazy. She didn't feel fully conscious. Her body was weak, and she couldn't move at all.

As she was blinking with half-lidded eyes, a nurse who happened to be there noticed her. Learning she had awoken, the nurse left the room in a hurry.

The nurse returned with three doctors. Clad in white coats, the doctors touched the girl's motionless body and shone lights on her to check her reactions. This sort of behavior ended after about fifteen minutes.

It had to be about an hour since her awakening.

She still couldn't move, but she was clearly conscious. Her vision had sharpened, and she could distinctly see the patterns on the cream-colored ceiling.

A man in a military uniform came into the room.

He was a skinny man with black hair and irises like dots.

Sparkling on his chest was the proof that he had killed a great many dragons: a gray Order of Great Balmung. The rank insignia on his collar indicated that he was a commodore. Though the girl didn't understand such things at this point in time.

The man's eyes had the particular violent gloom of one who had seen much darkness. His irises were black, too. The deep wrinkles carved into his forehead also expressed that the life he had led had not been a peaceful one.

The man said to her, "It's been a long time... Or so I'm told."

He spoke in the human tongue, not the True Language.

But the girl was able to understand what those words meant. The True Language, which the girl had spoken until that day, was the root of all languages of the world. Understanding the True Language meant being fluent in every language of the past—and into the future. The language the man spoke was a high-status language used only by the upper classes in Norvelland, but the girl understood it without difficulty.

But even knowing what he was saying, whether she would attempt to communicate with him was a completely different issue.

Her body moved on its own.

Previously, her body hadn't listened to her at all, but now it moved before her brain could even give the order.

Leaping from the bed like a spring, the girl flung herself at the dot-eyed man.

This is the man who killed the dragon.

She meant to smash the man's composed face with her right arm—the arm that had bandages wrapped around it. She was going to unleash a beating with a speed and force one would never expect from an injured girl. She was moving faster than the human eye could detect.

The man blocked the strike with one hand.

He caught the girl's arm like a winding snake, forcing her facedown on the floor.

And then the girl couldn't move at all.

In terms of pure strength, the girl had to be stronger. The girl had been bathed in the dragon's blood, and she had eaten the fruits of Eden. Her body was, in both appearance and substance, close to perfect.

The man, on the other hand, was too thin—sickly, even—and didn't look like he was very strong at all.

But despite that, the girl couldn't stand up against him.

"Don't ignore me when I speak, woman." The man's voice was

mechanical, and there was a force behind it that would brook no argument. "If you are greeted, then you respond with a greeting. Didn't your parents teach you that? Oh, I suppose they didn't…"

The girl decided to silently listen to him. That was all she could do.

"Then I'll introduce myself to you… But…you may remember me," he continued.

The girl had hardly any memory of the time when she'd been in the human world.

"I am Sigebert Siegfried. I am the head of the dragon-killing clan, Siegfried."

But she could still vaguely remember some things.

For example, the portrait that had decorated the great hall of her estate. It had been of the head of the family, whom she had not met even once, being one of so many children.

Her father.

That was who Sigebert Siegfried was.

"That look. It seems you do remember, after all…erm, Brunhild."

Brunhild Siegfried.

That had been the girl's name until she was three years old.

The girl who was the daughter of a dragon, who had been showered with the blood of the dragon, had belonged a family of dragonslayers.

"I am not Brunhild. I have no name."

The dragon's words echoed in her mind.

Ever since the dragon had said <I will call you *you*,> Brunhild had abandoned her name.

"I will continue, Brunhild." Sigebert went on, as if to trample upon her unspoiled memories. "I don't remember you at all. I didn't even know I had a daughter named Brunhild until the attack on Silver Island was over."

"I don't know any Siegfried."

Sigebert rolled up the sleeve of his left arm. There was a tattoo of a crest on his wrist. "There is one just like this on your left wrist. You are most definitely of the Siegfried bloodline. I have already conducted an inquiry. You were kidnapped thirteen years ago…daughter."

It was difficult to feign ignorance any longer. "So then what? You can't mean to have me inherit the Siegfried family name?"

"I do."

It didn't sound like he was joking.

"Don't you worry. Our shared blood is not enough for me to feel anything for you. But everyone has been hounding me to choose a successor," he said wearily. "I can make a guess as to how you were raised. After being taken to Silver Island, you were bathed in a dragon's blood…and raised by a dragon. Imagine…pretending to be family," Sigebert spat.

Enraged, Brunhild tried to move, but with him on her back, her struggling was futile. It was the most she could do to twist her neck around, glare at Sigebert, and groan, "It wasn't pretend."

Sigebert's expression as he looked down at her was complicated. "Sachs said if I talked to you, you'd understand… But it's no use. Not after being away for thirteen years. Or is it because that hair color is the opposite of mine?" he said carelessly, completely disregarding Brunhild's anger.

"Why…? Why can't I move…?"

"…Hmm?"

She clenched her teeth and tried to twist around, but she couldn't even do that.

"Ah. I'll tell you. You'll never beat me, no matter how long you live. You have no choice…but to submit." Sigebert started to unravel the bandage that was wrapped around Brunhild's right arm.

A chill ran up Brunhild's spine.

She recalled her final memory on the island.

Brunhild had failed to shield the dragon, and her body had been blasted apart. She had lost the right side of her chest and her right arm.

So then…

…why did she have a right arm now?

"It really does look draconic—reptilian, at the very least."

Humans who had been showered with the blood of dragons gained a superior ability to heal themselves. But it was impossible to regenerate flesh that had been lost.

"You can't win because I am a dragonslayer…" The bandages slithered and fell to the floor. "…and you are a dragon."

"Ah—ahhhhhhh!"

A dragon's arm was growing out from the scar where her right shoulder had been torn off.

"Isn't that nice? You get to be together."

"No! No, no, no! I—! I…!"

"What are you prattling about…? Your mouth was absolutely filthy with it…"

She remembered drinking the dragon's blood that had soaked into the beach.

To prevent them from having *it*. The only thought in her mind had been, *He's mine.*

She had drank, and drank, and drank, and drank.

This right arm was the result.

"What an unsightly girl."

Her vision went red.

"I'll kill you! I'll kill you, you bastard!!"

"I feel the same. I want to kill you. A stranded girl from an Eden… You're no daughter of mine. You're nothing more than a monster. However…"

Sigebert could not kill Brunhild. His reputation was on the line. The military and the research institutions had decided that Brunhild was a creation of Eden—one of the first things they had managed to recover from an island without having it turn to ash. There were already discussions of putting her in custody and adding her to the military registry.

"If you hadn't killed the dragon, then I never would have suffered this humiliation!" she cried.

"…What a fine attitude," the man sneered.

Noticing the cries, a doctor rushed in. After they yelled, "Sedatives," she felt a needle being thrust into her left arm. In the next moment, she felt her consciousness slipping.

Sigebert turned his back to Brunhild and started to leave.

"Mark my words…," she moaned. "I'll kill you… No…matter…

where you try to run… I'll take…revenge…for my father…with these hands…"

The strength rapidly faded from her body.

Turning just his head back, Sigebert said, "You're free to try to kill me. Though, I don't think your *father* would want that."

Her consciousness was too dim, and all sound was fading rapidly.

But…

Don't speak like you know what's best for me.

…even with her awareness fading, she could clearly hear what he said.

Her mouth wouldn't move.

She couldn't reply.

The sound of his military boots could no longer be heard.

Sigebert left the hospital.

The plan was to head to a port town within the day for the conquest of the next Eden.

But when he cut across the hospital garden, he ran into a black-haired boy.

His hair and eyes were the same color as Sigebert's.

He was a seventeen-year-old boy.

His name was Sigurd Siegfried, and he was Sigebert's son.

Sigebert came to a stop in front of his son. But he didn't say anything. No—he couldn't.

Sigebert was no good at talking to people. He would rarely ever initiate conversation with anyone. He was the same with his son, but this was a different breed of reticence.

Sigurd gave him an accusatory look with the wide black irises that resembled those of his deceased mother so much.

Sigebert didn't know what to say. Dealing with his dragon daughter had been far easier than this.

Sigurd seemed to tire of waiting and began himself. "…So you went to see Brunhild."

"…I did."

Sigurd was in his rebellious phase, so he never addressed his father with proper respect. But that was just as well.

"You're heading to the port without stopping by home?"

"…That's right."

Sachs had said that there was an invisible bond between parent and child.

Sigebert thought that was true. Whenever he spoke with his son, for some reason, he struggled with his words far more than normal.

"So they're putting her in the military register and taking her into custody? And giving her a rank?"

"…That's right."

"You were never that considerate with me, though."

Sigurd was also in the military, as a sergeant. It was a high rank, uncommon for one so young, but nepotism played no part in his achievements. There was a tendency for everyone to assume that Sigurd had succeeded due to pressure from the Siegfried family, but at the very least, the head of the family had never exerted any pressure that they accommodate him.

Sigurd had started as a private and achieved the rank of sergeant all on his own.

Sigebert knew that Sigurd had worked hard.

But…

"…Quit the army," he said icily. "Killing dragons…is not as fun as you think it is."

Sigurd took one step toward Sigebert. It looked as if he had stopped himself from grabbing his father by the cuff. "I have to show you what I'm capable of…or you won't let me inherit the name of dragonslayer!"

"No matter how hard you work…you'll never inherit the name…nor the Balmung… Not you."

"Not *me*?"

Sigurd sensitively picked up on the meaning behind his words. "You can't mean to suggest that Brunhild…"

"…It's possible."

"…Why? …Why would you hand them to someone who's been absent from the family for thirteen years?" Sigurd was so angry it seemed like he couldn't even speak anymore.

Sigebert didn't know what to say. So he left his son behind and headed to the port city.

"I'm not giving up on the military!" His son's voice came at him from behind. "I'll prove to you that I'm better than her! Then when I do...!"

Pretending he couldn't hear his son's voice, the father left.

Johann Sachs was a colonel in the Norvelland army.

He had enlisted at the same time as Sigebert Siegfried, and they were the same age as well. But that was where the similarities ended. In just about every other respect, they were total opposites.

Sigebert was a violent man of few words. He was a rationalist and always took the shortest possible route to his goal.

Sachs was a jovial chatterbox. He was optimistic and believed that one of life's greatest pleasures was traveling.

Another might have viewed their friendship as the most unlikely pairing, but perhaps it was *because* they were polar opposites that they could find areas in which to complement each other.

Since one was a rationalist and the other an optimist, one would naturally have an easier time ranking up than the other, but that didn't bother Sachs. He wasn't a man to attach a lot of importance to status. In fact, he even thought of it as a hassle.

This was the sort of man Sigebert sought to make a request of.

It wasn't anything unusual. Sigebert and Sachs had a give-and-take relationship. If he happened to receive work in an area he wasn't the most proficient in, he would seek his friend's aid without a second thought. That was a much quicker solution than worrying over it or trying to figure it out on his own. Since they were polar opposites, if there was something Sigebert couldn't do, Sachs surely could.

Sigebert most commonly required Sachs's assistance in fields requiring sociability.

When training their juniors and correcting those soldiers who were capable but had problems, Sigebert would try to resolve things with violence. Violence would settle things for the moment, but it was far from a fundamental solution.

This was usually where the sociable Sachs stepped in, but…

"Aghhhhhhhhhhhhhhhhhhhhh…" Sachs let out a big yawn in the car as it headed to the hospital for pickup. It startled the driver, and he looked at Sachs through the mirror.

The problem child this time was on another level entirely.

She has the blood of a dragon and was raised by a dragon, but she hails from a famous clan of dragonslayers… And on top of all that, she's a sixteen-year-old girl…? You've got to be kidding me.

Sachs restrained the urge to paw at his scalp. He'd gone through the trouble of gelling and styling his hair, so he couldn't ruin it. First impressions were particularly important with girls, after all. Since he was already old enough to be considered middle-aged, Sachs cared much more about making the right first impression than the average man.

The name of this problem child was Brunhild Siegfried.

She was the girl who had been retrieved the month before, during the mission to take Silver Island.

By Sachs's analysis, there were four problems.

First, the dragon's blood.

It was publicly known that dragon's blood was a deadly poison that had about a 99 percent chance of killing a person if it so much as touched their skin. However, even if they were lucky enough to survive, there was also the risk of it causing severe mental decline. This particular side effect was not very well understood outside of military personnel, medical staff, scholars, and researchers.

In Sachs's estimation, the girl had, in all likelihood, suffered a similar mental affliction.

That had to be the case. Otherwise, she wouldn't be calling herself the daughter of a dragon. This self-identification was the second problem. Or was it? He'd heard the story of a girl being raised by wolves before. Perhaps, under unique circumstances, calling oneself the child of a beast *wasn't* the most outlandish thing…?

Then, there was the third problem… Running counter to her barbaric upbringing, they said her bloodline was of the esteemed Siegfried family. Ridiculous.

She just so happened to be the daughter of a man without peer.

Even if I am a close friend, would you really ask me to take care of your own daughter just because you're bad at communicating with her? She's your daughter! *At least* try *to have a civil conversation with her! You're parent and child.* So he had persuaded the busy Sigebert to stay in the city until Brunhild had awoken.

After Brunhild had woken up, Sachs had had Sigebert go visit her in the hospital.

He didn't know what sort of conversation they'd had.

On Sigebert's return, he had said in his usual dour tone, "…It's no use. I can't deal with her, and I refuse to. I want her put down."

Come now, that's a bit much, don't you think? Maybe it's because you haven't seen her in thirteen years… Well, actually, considering how the Siegfried family operates, it was probably your first time meeting her… But you're still her father, aren't you? You should never say that you want her "put down"!

Sachs was typically a mild-mannered guy, but he snapped then. He had yelled at his friend and was prepared to get physical.

And so Sigebert decided to foist Brunhild off on Sachs. He'd said, "You're the one who retrieved her from Eden, and you're the one who's actually worried about her. Any way you slice it, you're far more fatherly than me."

Stroking his carefully groomed beard, Sachs considered this.

…Don't you dump this on me.

Johann Sachs knew Sigebert Siegfried.

The world knew him as a heroic dragonslayer. This was a fact. The conquest of the Edens wouldn't be possible without him.

But Sachs thought that Sigebert's true weapon was his power of insight. His small irises were always fixed on the nature of things.

He would surely rise to the top of the military—with his shrewd intuition as his weapon.

"But you know, Sigebert…," Sachs grumbled. "This is one of those rare instances where I think you're mistaken…"

Even if I was the one to save her, and no matter if I've been worried about her…

You're her father, Sigebert.
Not me.

He stepped out of the car and entered the hospital.

Before heading to the room where Brunhild Siegfried was staying, he checked his appearance in the mirror. Even if he was going to be speaking with the child of a dragon, she was still a girl.

He carefully adjusted his bangs, which were just long enough that they wouldn't fall into his eyes. Not bad, not bad at all. Sachs had been a handsome man in his youth.

It was no exaggeration to say that he'd been quite the ladies' man.

With age, the vitality and vibrancy of his younger days had left him, but he'd developed a face that gave a sense of his broad-minded character, and he had no shortage of secret admirers in the military.

But Sachs wasn't in a relationship.

There was something he refused to forget.

There had been an incident that occurred during the winter of his twenty-fourth year. After being stabbed by a woman he was seeing, and rushed to emergency care, he had cut off all relations with women.

Girls were scary.

Finishing the final check of his personal grooming, he muttered, "All right." He had himself psyched up.

He tucked a dagger, his favored weapon, into his pocket.

Just in case.

If she saw herself not as a human, but as the daughter of a dragon, there was a nonzero chance that he would be attacked. Even if he was more good-natured than Sigebert, though not as strong, Sachs was still a capable military officer.

Although, from what I've heard about her upbringing, it doesn't seem like I'd stand a chance against her...

He didn't need the dagger.

The windows of the private room were wide open. The curtains fluttered and swayed in the breeze.

Brunhild Siegfried was sitting up in bed. Her silver hair appeared

red in the sunlight. Her eyes were like a smoldering bonfire in the quiet dark.

Black flames lingered there, in the shape of a person.

That was Sachs's impression of Brunhild Siegfried. Even noticing that he had visited the room, Brunhild didn't give him so much as a glance.

"Brunhild Siegfried—is that you?"

She reacted. But the moment of her reaction was not when he called her the name *Brunhild Siegfried*, but when he said "you."

"Don't call me 'you,' human."

Her reaction to the term of address confused him, but he wasn't going to pry. From experience, Sachs knew that fixations and hang-ups about names were often due to reasons only that person would understand.

"So then… What should I say?"

"Who are you?"

Damn, he thought. It was common decency to introduce yourself before asking someone else their name.

Sachs raised his eyebrows and lifted the corners of his lips gently. His winning smile never failed to lower the guards of people he interacted with—at least, that's how it went with humans…

"Apologies, my name is Johann Sachs. I'm a colonel in the Norvelland army and an old friend of Sigebert's."

He checked to see how she would react upon hearing Sigebert's name. His idea had been to use a mutual acquaintance as a key to opening up the conversation. It seemed that had succeeded. Brunhild's eyebrows twitched.

"Where is that man?" she demanded, hostile.

No surprise there. Sigebert had killed the dragon.

"At sea, I believe. I'm not sure, either." Colonel Sachs had been ordered by Commodore Sigebert that under no conditions was he to give away his location.

Staring at Sachs with deep-crimson eyes, the girl declared, "That's a lie," as if she had read his mind. "Why are you lying?"

Sachs knew how to counter at times like these.

He put on an awkward smile, as if he were at a loss. "It's not a lie. He travels the oceans of the world looking for Edens. I imagine only his fellow seafarers will know where he is."

The eerie girl narrowed her eyes and looked at Sachs for a while, but she just said "I see" in resignation, then averted her eyes.

She was still again, like a doll.

"Sigebert has asked me to handle y—…matters, Brunhild." Just as Sachs was about say "you" again, he caught himself.

She wouldn't react anymore. So he continued to talk at her. "Sigebert is busy, and he can't be in the capital for a while."

He kept the tone of his voice as soft as possible so as to not irritate her. After all, this girl had already bared her fangs against Sigebert, a man lauded as the strongest in the Norvelland army.

"Isn't there anything you'd like to ask about? For example, your current situation, or what comes next, or about being put on the military register, anything."

"I don't care." She was blunt.

"You don't have any problems—like maybe you don't want blood drawn, or did it hurt to have the scales on your right arm peeled off? I could negotiate with the doctor."

Brunhild, a living fruit of Eden.

Though they weren't technically doing any human experimentation, every day they gathered and analyzed the components of all the substances that comprised her body. This was the reason she was still not discharged, despite her wounds being largely healed. Apparently, they were also doing tests of her physical and mental abilities as well, but she'd been extremely uncooperative, and things were not going well. She had endured a sudden attack by humans and been driven from her home. It was no wonder she didn't want to cooperate with them.

"Examine and test me as you see fit, so long as I'm able to do the one thing I need to do."

I must kill that man, she said.

Though Sachs didn't affirm her desire to kill his friend, neither did he reject it. "I understand the feeling painfully well. Your family was killed. Of course you'd want to exact revenge. But…that kind of…open hostility isn't a very good idea."

"Not a very good idea…?"

"I mean, it's not like everyone in the world is your enemy. It may seem like that right now, and there's no helping that. But I want you to understand, bit by bit, that it's not like that."

There were some who had proposed that they toss Brunhild into a research facility, as if she were a lab animal.

But others had opposed that, and exercising the art of negotiation to the utmost, they had somehow reached the point where the military was taking her into custody.

That was Sachs's doing. He wasn't going to loudly declare that he was on her side, but he wanted to help out this sixteen-year-old girl as much as he could.

…He couldn't help but see his own daughter in her.

"I'll leave for now."

Their brief meeting was at an end.

He had to take his time to carefully melt the wall of ice between them…

She was in a delicate state right now.

"Well then, till next time."

Sachs began to visit the hospital regularly.

Although, even after his visits became more regular, it would be a while yet before there were any major developments.

Whenever Sachs spoke to her, she would either ignore him or just give curt responses.

To be frank, she was creepy.

She would just stare at him with those dark-red eyes, as if she was studying him.

But after a full week, the girl initiated conversation.

She said she was reconsidering a little—she spoke in a polite manner.

"It was only for four days, but I did spend some time in the outside world…once… To my dismay, I ascertained that there is no place in this world where dragons may live peacefully. Being the daughter of a dragon, if I am to survive in this world, then I must acclimate to human society— live as one myself."

Sachs's eyes widened. After being open-mouthed for a while…

"You're using such difficult words..." the thought slipped out of him.

There was no helping that. Who would have been able to imagine that a human raised by a dragon would manage such refined vocabulary and polite language?

"I was granted knowledge in Eden."

There was still a wall between them. Impossibly high and frozen solid.

But Sachs was pleased to see that she was beginning to warm up, even if only a little.

"As you say," she continued, "from my perspective, everything in this world is my enemy. But you've been friendlier to me than others. You seem to be the only person I can rely on."

For the first time, the girl said his name, "Sachs." She asked, "*Can* I rely on you?"

He had prepared no response other than, "Of course."

Brunhild had said, "I require knowledge on the human world, in particular, this 'military' among which I will be living."

For whatever reason, she had the ability to read, so he decided to give her books. At first, he brought her three books for children, but by the next day, she had finished them all.

And as soon as she saw Sachs's face, she said this:

"Sachs, next time please bring me something of a higher level."

In a single day, she finished reading the five introductory books that he brought next.

Now he was bringing in nothing but academic texts.

But the girl's words became gentler, as if in inverse proportion to the difficulty of the books.

It seemed like she was learning something important through regular conversation with Sachs.

With each passing day, the number of books around her increased. She wanted to read books on the history of the nation and politics, and about military affairs, so he ordered his subordinates to bring them to her.

The girl became absorbed in books about the military with which she was affiliated.

She looked so intent and single-minded.

These days, there was no one this earnest among the trainees. She worked a hundred times harder than Sachs had when he was young. He often found her so absorbed in her reading that he would hesitate to even enter the room.

But Sachs was just a little worried.

Solely reading textbooks day in and day out would do nothing to open her heart. She would grow up to become an antisocial bookworm.

With that thought in mind, he tucked a certain book in between the academic texts and dropped off the stack.

It was a story of a girl who had been raised by wolves.

The girl who had lost her wolf parents was invited back into the human world. The wolf girl was confused at first, but being touched by kindness, she gradually grew used to humans, and in the end, she lived with people. It was a happy ending.

There were distinct parallels between the life of the girl in the story and the life of Brunhild.

Sachs wanted that happy ending for Brunhild as well.

The next day, from the window on the door to her hospital room, he happened to see Brunhild reading that very story.

Tears were streaming down her cheeks.

That day only, he withdrew without trying to speak to her.

He'd heard it said that silver dragons had beautiful hearts.

Was it because she had spent time with that dragon that she was so beautiful and so innocent?

It was two weeks after he had begun visiting her.

"Please call me Brunhild," the girl said.

By this time, Brunhild's knowledge of the military had become quite significant.

"You're a colonel, Colonel Sachs. That's a high officer position. I don't know what sort of rank I'll be granted when I'm officially registered in

the military, but I doubt it will be higher than brigadier general. Since I'll be your subordinate, it would be strange for you to never address me directly. From now on, please call me Brunhild. And I will call you Colonel, rather than Sachs. And I will also speak with proper courtesy," the girl said.

"…Okay, sure."

The girl was slowly trying to become human.

To that end, she was trying to adapt to the rules of the human world. It seemed that lately she had also cooperated with the tests of her physical and intellectual abilities.

That's good to hear… But ever since she's started speaking politely and calling me Colonel, I've felt a little…lonely. Just a little.

It happened when Sachs was talking about a failure of his youth.

The girl hung her head just slightly, putting her hand to her mouth to hide it.

The corners of her mouth were gently upturned, and a pleasant giggle slipped out.

It was the first smile he had ever seen her make.

He'd understood it ever since he'd witnessed her cry over that story…

This girl was a human, and she had a human heart.

Though she looked quite mature and was smart, on the inside, it seemed she was a very authentic…sixteen-year-old girl.

They came to talk about many things.

"I'm written about in here."

That day, Brunhild had a three-page newspaper article spread out on top of the bed.

THE GIRL WHO CAME BACK FROM EDEN, THE LITTLE LADY WHO VAN-ISHED THIRTEEN YEARS AGO IS FOUND ON A DRAGON'S ISLAND, THE HOUSE OF THE DRAGONSLAYERS NOW HOUSES A DRAGON'S DAUGHTER, and other such shameless headlines popped out at him.

"Colonel, is the world aware of my existence?"

"…That's right. You're famous."

A gag order had been imposed within the military about the girl they had found on Eden, but you couldn't put doors on people's mouths. Word had leaked somehow, and a mole had brought that information straight to the press. Sachs hadn't wanted the girl to get worked up like this.

"I've heard that there is discrimination in the lands of men." The girl grabbed her bandaged right arm with her left hand. Her right arm was covered in dragon's scales. "If they see me as a dragon, I'm afraid to think of what they might do to me…"

"Don't worry. The world doesn't know about your right arm or about the fact that you were raised by a dragon."

"But the headlines are saying I'm a dragon's daughter."

"That's just newspaper companies making it look dramatic. It just happened to coincide with the facts. Hardly anyone believes it."

The only facts the military had publicized, after being hounded by reporters, was that "A daughter of the Siegfried family had been found on an uninhabited island."

"When I look out the window, I sometimes see a person with a camera… So those people are reporters?"

Sachs scratched at his head. "Yes… Though they're not allowed on hospital grounds…"

"Oh, really? There was even a reporter who came to my room in the middle of the night."

"What…? Are you serious?"

"Yes. There happened to be a nurse passing by at the time, and the person left in a hurry, but…" Brunhild clenched the white sheets covering the bed. "…It was scary."

"We'll try upping the security… But this might be the one thing I can't do anything about."

"So there are things even you have no control over, Colonel?"

"Yeah—like my senior officers or society in general. Sorry… But you'll just have to bear with it. For a few months."

"A few months?"

"Yeah, the people of this country are quick to heat up and quick to cool. I figure in a few months, they'll be all over someone else."

"Have there been people like me in the past?"

"There hasn't been anyone as unique as you, but there are plenty of people who have gotten as much public attention. People who have done bad things are attacked so much in the news you wouldn't believe it. But everything always blows over after a few months. Relax; in time, you'll be able to live a quiet life."

Brunhild fell into thought for a moment and then muttered, "…Attacked."

Brunhild looked at the colonel with her red eyes, filled with the light of curiosity, and said, "Colonel. Starting today, I'd like to read lots of newspapers."

They came to talk to each other about their personal histories.

A researcher had said to him, "I want you to ask her what sort of place that Eden was," but Sachs didn't give a damn about that. He decided that whatever she told him about Eden, he would tell no one else. He had gotten the feeling that talking would be a terrible betrayal.

"The lands of men are full of incomprehensible rules. It's confusing," she said.

"What sort of rules were there in Eden?" Sachs asked her.

"There were no rules. In Eden, all creatures are family. There, no living creature feels the need to take advantage of another, so there is no need for rules. Man and wolf can be united. A woman may love another woman. Men may grow their hair as long as they please. Though there is family, there is no family head—you may live your life as you choose, for there is no obligation. You don't need a uniform; you may wear whatever clothes you like. You won't be made to take them off because they're unsuitable for your station."

All these things seem impossible in the lands of men, Brunhild said with a wry smile.

"…Ah, but it seems there was one taboo."

She lowered her long white eyelashes. Her expression suddenly grew dark.

"A daughter may not love her father."

There was a tightness around Sachs's heart.

"Colonel, is that rule the same, even in the lands of men? Is a daughter not allowed to love her father?"

After folding his hands and taking a deep, secret breath, Sachs answered, "Not at all. I mean, a father and daughter are family. What's wrong with them loving each other?"

Sachs's answer caused Brunhild's lips to curl into an earnest smile. "In that one way, this land is freer than Eden."

"Indeed, it is. In fact, I'd say that the more he's loved by his daughter, the more blessed a father is. After all, it's more the norm for a girl to hate her father as she grows up."

"Was that how it was with your daughter, too?"

"Huh?" Sachs froze.

There was confusion in Brunhild's eyes. "I surmised from the way you spoke that you have a daughter of your own…"

"…Ah, mm-hmm." His words caught in his throat. "I did have a daughter. But in my case…it would be reasonable for her to hate me."

She must have inferred something from the look in Sachs's eyes…

…because Brunhild asked no further questions.

One month passed. Sachs visited the hospital just about every day.

"You have a lot of free time, Colonel."

His devotion seemed to bear fruit, as now they had a relationship where she would make slightly harsh jokes with him. Perhaps she had opened her heart just a little.

Incidentally, the colonel did not have a lot of free time.

He was working again that day. Brunhild's guardianship was an official order from the commodore. He was carrying out his duty right now.

"Isn't it lonely, having no one coming to visit you? Incidentally, your discharge day has arrived at last. I'm here to pick you up."

The research that required collecting tissue samples and bodily fluids and such from Brunhild had all concluded the day before. Afterward, the samples would continue to be studied and used in experiments with lab animals, but there was no further need for Brunhild to be in the hospital.

"If I'm being discharged, that means I'm going to be officially enlisted in the military today, doesn't it?"

Brunhild rose from the bed and stood at attention.

Sachs wanted to say, *You don't have to act so formal*, but he stopped himself.

He cleared his throat and then put on a very solemn expression. "First, from your letter of appointment...," he said, and brought out a piece of parchment from his bag. Even in the modern era with its developed paper-making technology, high-quality parchment was used for official documents. "...An officer, straight out of the gate, huh? Maybe I shouldn't say this, since it was my own proposal... But I didn't think it would actually go through... The influence of the Siegfried family never fails to surprise me."

He handed the parchment to Brunhild. Seeing what was written on it, she also seemed surprised.

Since it was stated that Brunhild would be appointed as a second lieutenant of the army.

Even if it was the lowest officer rank, her becoming an officer so suddenly was the culmination of various political circumstances converging at the exact right points.

The Eden research institutions were still insisting that Brunhild should be treated as a test subject. They were being completely unreasonable, saying that they would do repeated biological experiments on her and then dissect her at the end. And sadly enough, at first Brunhild's father, Sigebert, had agreed to this...

There was also a group who wished to see her accepted as a person. Most of the soldiers who had seen her in the conquest of Silver Island were of this camp. Witnessing her pitifully losing her right arm made those who were still trying to turn her into an experiment seem a little heartless. Sachs had insisted that although there could be benefits to running tests on her blood and tissue, afterward she should be taken into custody and put to use in the military—they could also observe her progress that way. Brunhild's incredible intellect and physical capabilities had been proven through various tests, and it would be a tragic waste to dissect and kill her.

Both factions were vying for dominance, but behind the scenes, Sachs had won over Sigebert and had caused him to withdraw the Siegfried family's backing from the side of the researchers. Trying to protect her from inhumane experiments by giving her a social position as an officer and making her existence official had been Sachs's plan from the start.

That had somehow gone well, and the girl had become a second lieutenant.

Of course, she was a second lieutenant in name only.

Sachs made his tone of voice hard. "It sounds bad to say, but that status is purely decorative."

This was the one thing he just had to let her know—even if the rank of second lieutenant was granted to her without her consent.

There were plenty of soldiers in this country who couldn't become second lieutenant, even if they had the appropriate skills and ambition. Or rather, it was largely like that. There were plenty among Sachs's subordinates. Considering their efforts, he had to let her know the fact that this was "decorative."

Even if she was from a distinguished family with a unique upbringing, it was fair to say that being suddenly designated an officer was blasphemy to other soldiers.

"Brunhild. The appropriate comportment is demanded of an officer. You absolutely cannot forget that."

"Understood," Brunhild said with a salute.

"Well then, as your superior officer, I will grant you your first mission. In two months, you will offer a speech to the environmental organization Typhon."

"A speech? If I'm in the military, then isn't fighting my job?"

"It would be easier for me if that were the case…" Sachs scratched the tip of his nose.

This was another example of various political circumstances converging at the exact right points.

The rank of second lieutenant would protect Brunhild from inhumane experimentation. Apparently, the plan of the research institutes right now was to say, *Okay, so we should just drag her down from that position.* Their scheme was to toss Brunhild at the environmental group Typhon.

Typhon called itself an environmental group, but it was, in fact, a fanatical religious group that worshipped dragons as the messengers of God.

This group's creed was the premodern idea that "after death, the souls of those who have done good deeds will be guided to paradise, called the Kingdom of Eternity by dragons, the messengers of God."

Typhon had for some time been repeatedly clashing with the Eden research organizations and the military. Their stance was fastidiously opposed to the conquest of Edens and killing dragons.

And then there was the reporting on the "daughter of the dragon" from all the newspapers.

There was no way Typhon would butt out of that. Since, to them, dragons were the messengers of God, they would not allow a mere human to call herself their daughter.

It had even leaked that this "dragon's daughter" would be enrolled in the military. Even an idiot would know where the information had leaked from, but…

The research organizations had ordered that the military take responsibility to clarify matters to Typhon. They were demanding that Brunhild explain why she had enlisted and also admit she was not the daughter of a dragon.

Making Brunhild a second lieutenant had already complicated things enough, so the military didn't have enough power left to reject this demand.

And so Brunhild's first mission as a second lieutenant was "to explain to a fanatical religious organization that she was not the daughter of a dragon"—she'd wound up with a task even more difficult than some half-baked military operation.

The research organizations envisioned this scenario: Either the girl would quit the military out of fear of Typhon's radicalism or she would be forcibly deposed on the grounds that she had "failed to deliver an appropriate speech."

…But he couldn't explain all that to her.

There were still two months until the day of the Typhon address. He would feel bad about continually putting pressure on the girl for that whole time.

"Relax. You just need to talk to them. Take it easy. We'll rehearse it, too."

"Understood. I will do some research on the group called Typhon, as well."

"You don't have to put on such a brave front. Okay?"

It made him remember how earnest she had been when she had been in the hospital.

Even if she did her best to study and put everything into a speech, if it turned out that they were fanatics who wouldn't listen... Such an outcome would be an unfathomable shock to her.

But this was surely the first step. He wanted her to overcome it, somehow.

Over the past month, Brunhild had sometimes smiled at him during their casual conversations. He wanted her to be able to smile like that in front of others, too.

He wanted the day to come when Brunhild could smile normally, like a human. That was Sachs's honest wish.

After being discharged from the hospital, Brunhild started moving to a certain estate. It was the residence of the Siegfried family. The date and time of her discharge was told only to limited parties, herself included. This was to deal with the mass media. It seemed efforts paid off, as Brunhild was not exposed to a barrage of questions from reporters and was able to quietly get into her welcome car.

The Siegfried estate, despite being situated right in the middle of the city, had a large rose garden and combat training grounds.

In front of the large gates, a great line of servants stood to welcome Brunhild's arrival.

"...Ah..." With a confused expression, Brunhild looked between Sachs, who accompanied her, and the servants.

"How charming," Sachs said with a smile. "Well, that would be a surprise... To be greeted by this many servants after living on an uninhabited island."

She had this kind of childlike side to her.

"I wonder what I should do…," she said.

"Stand tall and proud. This place is your home." Sachs lightly tapped her back. Brunhild staggered forward. "This is as far as I go. From here on out, I've left matters to the people of this household."

Brunhild turned back to Sachs. "Thank you for everything." And then she bowed her head deeply.

Once again, he thought, *She really is a good girl; she's become such a good girl.*

"Um, Colonel. May I ask one final thing?"

"Sure. What is it?"

"I would still like you know if you could tell me where Commodore Sigebert is."

She said she wanted to apologize for her rudeness when she first met him.

Sachs hesitated.

The girl had asked that very question when they first met—saying she would kill Sigebert. There was no way he could have told her then.

But now…things might be different. She had softened up quite a bit in the past month. When she said she wanted to apologize, it didn't sound like a lie.

But…

"He's always been a wanderer. He doesn't tell me where he goes, either." He laughed it off.

It wasn't that he didn't believe this girl.

It was just that he had made a promise to his friend. He had been told that under no circumstance was he to reveal his friend's location to Brunhild.

I'm the only friend he has… A betrayal would shatter him.

Even if Brunhild had become a good girl, he couldn't break his promise.

"I see."

Brunhild gave a charming smile.

"Well, if he does contact you, I'd be glad if you told me."

Brunhild bowed.

"Yeah. I'm sure he will," Sachs said, and then left the estate.

The officers of the Norvelland Imperial Army were lazy.

A lot of them were night owls since they could wake up at whatever hour in the morning they pleased.

A lot of them were dilettantes, too. They would draw illustrations or write poetry during their working hours.

Those who went from civilian to soldier would wake up early and train hard, but the officers spent that same time snacking—while stroking their ever-swelling bellies.

Nobody said anything.

Officers came from the aristocracy. The only ones who could complain about them were the royal family, the archbishop, or other aristocrats, but they never did such a thing since their highest priority was maintaining the status quo and protecting their own comforts.

Officers truly devoted to their duties were in the minority. It was people like Sigebert Siegfried and Johann Sachs who held the nation of Norvelland together.

The servants of the Siegfried household had also assumed that Brunhild would be living a leisurely lifestyle—and that the rank of second lieutenant that had been given her was no more than an easy, temporary position.

Brunhild Siegfried looked like glass.

Her hair was platinum, her skin was pale, her hands were small, her fingers narrow. She seemed like she would break if you touched her.

No one could imagine that a girl who looked like that would voluntarily undergo harsh training.

She woke up early, followed the discipline that she had laid down herself, relentlessly brutalized her own body, hungrily devoured knowledge, and went to bed early.

She was sociable and mild-mannered. She was also so considerate of others that you would never imagine she had been raised on an uninhabited island. Not only was she close with the servants, she also never forgot to be respectful to them. So the servants came to want to return her kindness as much as they could.

But they were unable to grant her wish.

There was only ever one thing that Brunhild asked of the servants.

"Could you please tell me where my father, Lord Sigebert, is right now?"

They would have been happy to answer her…if they could. But they simply couldn't. Sigebert, the head of household, hadn't told anyone where his expedition would take him.

Though the rest of her body was as white as purely driven snow, there was fire in her eyes.

There were a number of soldiers of the Siegfried family bloodline at the estate, but none of them was as diligent as Brunhild.

Aside from one—Sigebert's son, Sigurd Siegfried.

Purely in terms of how hard he trained, Sigurd was even more demanding of himself than Brunhild.

Brunhild would go to bed early, but Sigurd skimped on sleep to train himself.

Sigurd was a seventeen-year-old sergeant. In order to be acknowledged by their father, he had started from the lowest rank and become a sergeant over the course of three years.

But despite that, they were saying Brunhild had suddenly become a second lieutenant. What's more, she was sixteen years old. And she was a *woman*.

Is this some kind of joke? Why would Father choose her over me…?

It was only natural that Sigurd would feel angry.

But even so, had Brunhild been a dimwit who only thought of her rank as easy and temporary, then Sigurd would have been able to accept her appointment. He wouldn't have had to take her seriously, thinking of her as another obstacle he would soon overcome.

But it seemed that not only was Brunhild diligent—she had talent.

"Second Lieutenant, ma'am."

One day, Sigurd approached Brunhild. The afternoon lecture from their attendant instructor was over, and when she left the room, Sigurd was deliberately there, waiting for her.

"Sergeant Sigurd." With her hair like platinum swaying, the girl looked at Sigurd.

"Oh, you remembered the name of a humble sergeant? What an honor."

"I have remembered the names of everyone starting from the rank of noncommissioned officer and above."

Noncommissioned officer.

In this nation, sergeant was the lowest rank among noncommissioned officers. In other words, that meant Sigurd was just barely worth Brunhild remembering him. Also, given that he was a lower rank than her, her respectful address came off as sarcasm. Even he knew that these thoughts sounded like he was cherry-picking faults, but he'd already made up his mind.

I don't like her.

Brunhild's lithe frame was clad in a new red military uniform.

"This is only if you have the time for it, ma'am, but would you be able to accompany me for my military martial arts training?"

"Military martial arts training? Why?"

What he really wanted was to use martial arts training as an excuse to beat the pulp out of Brunhild.

"I've heard that on the tests of physical ability at the military hospital, you scored quite high, especially in the area of martial arts. So while I don't know much, and my abilities are limited, if you could…"

Sigurd didn't truly believe his abilities were limited.

Though he was strong-willed and rowdy, among the soldiers who had enlisted with him, he had the highest grades in both his academics and martial arts.

"My martial arts are different from the formal military style," Brunhild explained. "I don't know whether it will be useful, but if you don't mind…"

The second lieutenant said her afternoon plans were packed with lectures and preparation for the formal address that had been assigned as her first mission. So it was decided they would meet at the training grounds at six in the evening.

The training grounds were lit by the setting sun. The ceiling was vaulted. Right in the middle of the broad space that evoked the image of a coliseum, Sigurd stood alone. He had been in the training grounds since about thirty minutes before they were going to meet.

Sigurd had changed into highly functional clothing for training. There was a fine layer of dust over his entire outfit. Sweat was dripping from his spiky black hair.

He had finished his warm-up. Physically, he was feeling great. Mentally, he was in perfect shape, too. Just thinking about slamming a fist into that composed face got him excited. He was ready to put on a show.

Second Lieutenant Brunhild appeared right on time.

Just like when he had seen her at noon, she wore a crisp military uniform.

That wasn't really a bad thing, though. Their uniform was also highly functional, so there wasn't anything strange about her coming dressed like that. But the book she carried under her arm—*History of the Environmental Group Typhon*—just what kind of joke was that?

Yep, I can't stand her.

If I don't defeat her, my father will never acknowledge me.

He adopted a fighting stance without another word.

That was the starting signal for their training—or newbie bullying, rather.

"Well, then," said the second lieutenant, and then an instant later…

…Sigurd was looking at the sky.

Huh? What's going on?

There was a stinging pain in the back of his head.

…What happened?

Second Lieutenant Brunhild was at his side, reading a book. Her red eyes noticed Sigurd.

"You lost consciousness."

"…Huh?"

What was she talking about?

"I used a choke hold on you. I applied pressure to a major artery in your neck. It stopped the oxygen from reaching your brain, and you lost consciousness."

…

In other words…

…I lost?

Without being able to do anything, without even knowing what she'd done…

He'd been beaten by this woman?

"B-bullshit!" Sigurd surged to his feet. "One more time! Fight me one more time! That was just a fluke!"

Blood rushed to his head, making him forget to speak politely to a superior officer. Though Brunhild wasn't the type to be bothered about that sort of thing.

"Let's leave it here for today," she said.

"What, you're running away?"

"No. Intense exercise before bed affects my sleep, so I'd rather not."

Now that she mentioned it, the red sky of twilight had become a starry night.

"How…how long was I out?"

Perhaps from the brisk night air, he felt his head cooling just a little.

"About one hour. The current time is just past seven. If you require additional training, we can meet here again tomorrow at the same time."

Brunhild closed her book and left the training grounds. There was not a single speck of dust on the back of her red military uniform.

"…Shit!"

The next day, he would absolutely make sure her uniform was filthy all over.

That day, Sigurd pushed and pushed and pushed his body as brutally as he could until late at night and then slept like the dead.

…But Sigurd couldn't win the next day, either.

Though perhaps one could consider it progress that, right before he passed out, he was able to see Brunhild approach him so close it was as if she would kiss him.

A moment later, he awoke to see the night sky again. It was one hour later.

And beside him, calmly reading a booklet, was Second Lieutenant Brunhild. The title was *Welcome to Typhon*. It was a pamphlet printed by a dangerous environmental group.

Oh yeah. She was going to do an address or something with Typhon soon. Apparently, she was going up against in him in her spare time while studying Typhon.

"If you still need training, we can go again tomorrow," she said.

The next thing he heard was the sound of a booklet being closed. As he watched her walk away, he noted that her uniform was as pristine as ever.

This new routine of theirs continued another seven times.

After their ninth sparring match, Brunhild mentioned something.

"Let's make today our last training session. I have other things I must do."

Sigurd couldn't even formulate a reply.

Sparring ten times… No, could you even call it sparring? Since he hadn't even been able to touch her.

To Brunhild, going up against him had been nothing more than a waste of her time.

"…Understood," Sigurd said, and then he went into a fighting stance.

Brunhild responded by taking her own fighting stance. Across all their matches, it was the first time she had done so.

"Since this is the last, I will also use formal military martial arts," she said.

She's mocking me.

He'd make her regret handicapping herself with military martial arts.

He could see Brunhild come close. He was able to actually see it this time.

Sigurd moved before he could think. When she approached, Sigurd drew back the same distance. If it seemed like she was going to attack, he meant to strike her back instead, but Brunhild wasn't that careless. She anticipated Sigurd's counterattack, and then she drew back as well, too.

Dust billowed, dirtying her military boots.

He started over.

This time, Sigurd was the one to attack.

He was just like an arrow of lightning.

He closed the distance in a flash and struck. This was Sigurd's specialty, which he'd even used to knock out his instructor. The move pushed the human body to its limits.

But the girl dodged his lightning strike with a motion as graceful as moonlight. The sergeant's fist crossed with the second lieutenant's palm.

The glove fell from the girl's right hand.

The two of them glared at one another once more.

Today might be the day I win.

He felt his body temperature rising.

They clashed again, neither of them backing down.

And again.

…And again.

And then Sigurd realized something.

…She's holding back.

At first, he'd thought that all his efforts, going so far as to skimp on sleep, had borne fruit. He'd assumed his movements had become so efficient that Brunhild wasn't able to find an opening anymore.

But that wasn't it.

He was forced to realize that Brunhild had willfully ignored several opportunities where she could have definitely taken the advantage.

…Could it be that she's actually trying to train me, since this is our last match?

She was holding back on him. Simply fighting him with military martial arts was a handicap on its own, but to make matters worse, at this rate…

He didn't care anymore.

The spirit and power drained away from his stance.

Brunhild shot toward him and grabbed his neck with her right hand.

"Take everything from me, just like that," Sigurd muttered in desperation, and Brunhild stopped. She did nothing beyond grabbing Sigurd's neck.

"Take? Take what?"

"Everything," Sigurd said with self-deprecation. "Do you even know who I am?"

"You're Sergeant Sigurd."

"My name is Sigurd *Siegfried*. I'm Sigebert Siegfried's only son—and your elder brother."

Brunhild was doubtful. "His son…? If he has a son, then why would Commodore Sigebert want me to inherit the Balmung…?"

"It means he has no expectations of me," Sigurd spat desperately.

He had always suspected.

Ever since he had been allowed to join the military as a private.

It was just that he hadn't been certain, since Sigebert wasn't much of a talker.

He had put too much stock in the words *come crawling up from the very bottom*.

But you crushed that.

You just showed up out of nowhere and instantly became a second lieutenant.

He was suddenly painfully aware that she was special, and he wasn't.

…The inside of his mouth was salty.

No matter how much he put on a brave front, no matter how much effort he put in, if the identity that he had worked so hard to build up was suddenly shattered, despite how hard he had tried to maintain it this whole time…

Of course he'd want to cry.

"Why are you crying?" Brunhild asked.

"Do I really have to spell it out for you? Because I'm not going to do that."

His father's expectations, his father's favor, his father's gaze…

It was entirely possible that this perfectly flawless girl had no idea the significance of what she'd stolen from him.

But Brunhild's reply…

"I can understand your desires."

…was not what Sigurd had expected.

"What I can't understand is why *you're* crying—and not me."

Her tone changed.

…*Who is she?*

The ethereal woman he'd met at the estate—the girl like glass—was gone.

Sigurd realized his words had incurred her wrath.

Her nails were digging into him.

Surely, this was who she really was…

"Your father stole my father from me," she said. "He put me somewhere I didn't want to be and foisted upon me a position I never asked for."

I'm the one who wants to cry.

Her grip around his neck tightened. This was not the strength of a young girl. There was pressure on his respiratory tract, forcing a pathetic sound out of him.

"You're his son. If I kill you, will he be sad? Will that man be able to experience the despair I felt, the dark feelings I still harbor? Tell me…"

Her red eyes, which had shone like garnets before, now burned like hellfire.

"Gah…guh…"

With his consciousness fading, Sigurd forced the words out. "He'd be… sadder…"

"What?"

"Sadder…if you died…than if I…did…"

Brunhild's eyes widened just a little. The blazing flames flickered, then went out.

Her grip loosened.

Coughing, Sigurd swiped away Brunhild's hand.

Her glove off, Brunhild's right hand was covered in silver scales, though he hadn't noticed that while they were fighting.

"That…hand of yours…"

Only certain high officials were aware that Brunhild's right arm was that of a dragon. Of course, Sigurd had no idea.

What Brunhild had just said flashed through Sigurd's mind.

Her words of deep resentment—*"Your father stole my father from me."*

Surely the *father* Brunhild had spoken of wasn't—

"I am the daughter of a dragon," the girl said.

He had thought for sure that she had been living an easy life. No... He had wanted to think that. Because he had hated her.

"Do you...like your father?" Brunhild asked with hesitation.

If he had been asked this question a few seconds ago, Sigurd wouldn't have been able to answer.

But now.

"...I do. I respect him. I wish I could be a strong dragonslayer like him."

"...Even a father like that... Even that kind of man has a child who loves him?"

Even Sigurd was aware that Sigebert Siegfried's Balmung Cannon had killed the silver dragon. So even if she called him "*a father like that*," he didn't try to defend him.

"I...like my father, too," she said.

He didn't even have to guess at the "father" she was referencing.

"I...suppose I should apologize," she continued.

But though he considered why Brunhild would have to apologize, he still didn't get it.

"...But how should I put it? Human language is so inconvenient...," Brunhild said, then left the training grounds.

Even seeing her military uniform all dirty, Sigurd felt nothing.

For some reason, his frustration, anger, and jealousy were all gone now.

Perhaps it was because he had perceived the complex worries inside the girl who had looked so perfect to him.

Learning that she was also a creature who had feelings just like him, Sigurd felt a strange sense of affinity.

The following afternoon, Sigurd headed to Brunhild's room carrying a gift of apology for having lashed out at her repeatedly the past few days.

He knocked on the door. A ladylike voice replied, "Come in."

Brunhild was sitting at a round table where her lunch had been spread out on a white cloth. The maid at her side had just finished preparing her meal.

"Second Lieutenant… As an apology for my rudeness these past few days…"

"What is there to apologize for?"

"Well…"

…He didn't like how polite she was. It felt like she was erecting a wall between them.

And after the day before…when she'd spoken in what was surely her natural tone, it had sounded even more like she was rejecting him.

Brunhild gave the maid an eye signal. The maid picked up on that and bowed, then left the room.

"It seemed difficult to talk with a maid present."

"Oh, but there was no need…"

Her red eyes studied him. It was as if they were trying to see through to his depths… It made him want to flinch.

"…You're my superior officer. There's no need for you to speak politely with me," he said.

"I see. So it's my manner of speech." She immediately switched the way she spoke. Was that her quick wit, or was it a woman's intuition? "There's no need for you to speak politely with me, either. You can be more casual."

"I can't do that…"

"I've cleared the room out, though."

The haughty nature of her words irritated him. But he felt like he could see what she really thought better than when she spoke with such mechanical politeness, so perhaps this was better.

It had only been around two weeks since Brunhild had come to this estate, but she seemed thoroughly familiar with it. She was so expert it was as if she had been living here ever since she was born. It would do no good for Sigurd to be constantly on edge around her.

"Then I'll accept your offer." Huffing through his nose, he approached Brunhild's table. She pulled out the open chair and prompted him to sit, and Sigurd responded, taking a seat.

Right as Sigurd was about to hand Brunhild the apology gift—

"Will you eat this for me?" she said.

"Huh?"

With her gloved right hand, Brunhild pointed to the lunch spread atop the tablecloth.

"I don't like the taste of any of this. It's a hassle to have to eat these foods every day."

"You don't like the taste…? But it was all prepared by our family chef."

The Siegfried family chef was particularly talented personnel, head-hunted from a restaurant of excellent repute in the nation. Of course, everyone's tastes were different… But still, was it truly possible that none of the five items lined up on the table suited her palate?

"I can't understand human dining. Why do you subject your foods to such meticulous processing? It's vulgar." Her red eyes were looking down at a jelly made from apples and yellow peaches. "On the island, I ate fruit straight from the tree."

"Then couldn't you just ask for the fruit to be served as is?"

"It's no use. Their ingredients aren't any good to begin with. I tried eating a fruit from the human lands, but it was like eating sand."

Silver Island had been full of lush fruit. For Brunhild, no food found in the lands of men could hope to agree with her.

"But you'll pass out if you don't eat anything."

"No need to worry. I've supplied this body with enough calories to keep it moving, all while enduring insufferable flavors."

…Sigurd felt that he suddenly had a better understanding of why this woman was "special" to his father. He felt like her oddly pragmatic way of thinking was just like his.

"By the way, what's that?" Brunhild's gaze was on the bag Sigurd clasped. It was wrapped with a cute ribbon.

"Ohh, well, this is…"

"I would guess that it's an apology gift for me."

"Well, yeah… But I can't really give it to you now."

"Why not?"

"…It's food."

There were cookies inside.

He had lined up early that morning to buy some sweets that he'd heard were popular with noble ladies. Of course, if he'd wanted, he could have sent servants to do that, but he had gone himself as part of his penance. Even so, it was embarrassing to be the only man in line.

"I'll buy you something else later to make up for it. So…"

Before he was done talking, Brunhild snatched the cookies from him. She roughly tore open the wrapping with her slender fingers and pulled out a cookie.

"I see…"

Her pink lips parted. She took a small bite of the edge of the cookie.

She moved her little jaw a number of times, chewing thoughtfully. Then she took another small bite.

"…Do you like it?" Sigurd asked.

"It's dreadful. Is this dust shaped into a block?" she said as she took another bite.

"You don't have to force yourself to eat it…"

"Some things may be disregarded, and some may not. Of the two, this is the latter. I'm consuming your feelings, not the cookie."

"…Don't you think that's a little embarrassing to say so plainly?"

"Everyone speaks their mind in Eden. There, no one can lie. The lands of men are so full of deceit that it was a struggle for me to get used to it."

"…Are you going to be okay doing the Typhon address, like that?"

"I am still studying Typhon assiduously, but, well, I don't believe there will be an issue. Sachs taught me how to lie." Brunhild pulled out a second cookie.

"Sachs…taught you…how to lie?"

"Hmm? Is there something wrong with what I just said?"

"…You're suddenly being brutally honest about a lot with me."

"I decided I would accomplish my goal without lying to you. I've drawn a line for myself, so to speak."

He was about to ask her what she meant by that, but before he could, Brunhild pulled out a third cookie and said, "Help yourself to my lunch. I would rather not endure these horrid flavors alone."

"It's not really suffering for me, though…," Sigurd said before tucking into the spread. It was actually quite good.

Watching the girl continue to eat the cookies, despite going on about how much she disliked them, Sigurd had a thought.

In some ways, she's like Father.

But at her core, she was likely his total opposite.

Sigurd finished her lunch and then stood from his seat as he said, "Good luck with the address."

"I'd like you to come eat my meal for me again," Brunhild called out to him when he was about to leave.

When he turned his head to look back at her, their gazes met. She lowered her eyes, then added with a dulled edge to her voice, "You don't have to if you don't want to, though…"

He raised his right hand in place of a reply. Considering that he was attempting to make up for blowing up at her day after day, her request was trivial.

Every day after that, Sigurd went to eat her meals for her.

Brunhild's manner of speech was brusque and arrogant. She wasn't very expressive, either. But when Sigurd ate her meals for her, she would seem ever so slightly glad. The corners of her lips would turn up a little awkwardly. Sigurd thought these were far nicer than the sparkling smiles she showed the servants.

Brunhild could make skillful use of a public mask. But for some reason, with Sigurd, she would allow her true emotions to leak out. She was curt and rude, but because of that, Sigurd could be himself as well, and it felt comfortable.

Brunhild was famous, being in the newspapers, and was also held in high esteem by the servants. That she would only show her private face to Sigurd gave him an indescribable sense of superiority.

At first, he ate her meals for her as a form of apology.

But in time, he came to enjoy the visits.

During one of many meals together, Brunhild asked Sigurd, "Why is it the people of this estate don't know where their master is?"

Come to think of it, she had a point. Lately, Sigurd's father had seemed to vanish when he went out on expeditions. In the past, he had always told them which ocean he was venturing out on, at the very least. But this time, they weren't even supplied that much. Though even if they had known which ocean his vessel was on, it wasn't as if Sigurd could follow a warship floating on the high seas. That being the case, there wasn't much point in his father telling him where he was going anyway. That's why, until Brunhild had pointed it out, he hadn't noticed that his father never revealed his destination to him, either.

"You're his son, but even you don't know where he is?"

"…No, I haven't heard. With his line of work, he's hardly ever in the capital, after all. But he'll be back in a year."

"A year? Is he always gone that long?"

"If I'm being generous. He could be gone for as long as three."

Brunhild closed her eyes and clenched her left hand around her right shoulder. "That really is a long time…"

The Norvelland Empire was busy conquering Edens all over the world, and only Sigebert could operate the Balmung Cannon, which was needed for that goal. It was only natural that he would spend more time at sea than on land.

"The humans are always attacking dragons, even though dragons don't go out of their way to attack humans. You all should try getting attacked by a dragon sometime. Then you could understand the terror of it," Brunhild said, a very unsettling comment.

Was she planning to exact retribution on the city of Nibelungen? An act of revenge as the daughter of dragonkind?

"If you take out your anger on humanity, you're going to hell," he said. "That would involve not only Father but innocent civilians as well."

"Going to hell would pose a problem, indeed." Brunhild sighed.

Her jokes were hard to understand—and not funny in the slightest.

It was on a holiday.

Sigurd invited Brunhild to a movie.

"One of my hangers-on gave me two tickets," he said. "I don't want to waste them."

"I refuse. To be frank, I hate the city of Nibelungen. I don't even want to walk through it."

"But you might like what this movie's about." The corners of Sigurd's lips turned up.

Brunhild said dubiously, "Why?"

"It's a horror film," Sigurd said with pride. "A movie where humans are attacked by ghosts, one after another. Didn't you say that humans should try getting attacked, or something?"

"Oh, yes," Brunhild said, and then put a finger to her lips and considered it. After a short pause, she agreed with a little reluctance, saying, "Okay, fine."

Sigurd and Brunhild walked through the city together. Brunhild's eyes were on the ground the whole time they were walking to the movie theater. It was as if she didn't even want any of the sights of the city to enter her field of view.

The movie was neither good nor bad. Just as he'd been told, it was about ghosts picking off humans one by one. It was even a little lackluster for Sigurd, who had become something of a film buff.

He was slightly worried it might be boring Brunhild as well, so during the film, he stole a glance at her in the seat beside him out of the corner of his eye.

Surprisingly, she was watching the screen intently.

Fortunately, it seemed that Sigurd's worries had been groundless. The movie was a little dry, but Sigurd was fine with it as long as Brunhild was enjoying it.

After they left the theater, he asked Brunhild for her opinion.

"It was an interesting story," she said with an utter lack of charm.

"But, like, you must have…more opinions, right? For example…you thought it was scary, or it felt nice to see humans get killed…or something like that."

"I did have those thoughts, of course," Brunhild affirmed, but her look was quite clearly not that of a girl who was afraid of ghosts.

"It made me think of many things," she said, sounding philosophical.

"You weren't scared at all," Sigurd deplored.

But Brunhild hadn't been lying.

Later that night, Sigurd had finished up his daily training regimen and was about to return to his room, but just as he was passing through the Siegfried estate rose garden…

He caught sight of Brunhild.

The garden had lots of red flowers blooming. In the center of them was a girl sitting on the edge of the fountain. Her hair, normally silver, was dyed blue by the moonlight.

Perhaps it was because of the melancholy hue, but the girl looked lonely to Sigurd's eyes.

He approached Brunhild. She seemed to be lost in thought, and even when he came to stand beside her, she didn't seem to notice.

"What're you doing?" he addressed her, and Brunhild finally lifted her face.

"Hmm…? Oh…ah…"

It seemed she hadn't noticed him at all, and her words caught in her throat. It was a surprising reaction. The Brunhild Sigurd knew was a guarded woman. And now she was flustered and acting strangely.

Sigurd felt like an awkward silence was about to fall over them. So in place of Brunhild, who couldn't put any words together, Sigurd continued the conversation. "You usually go to bed so early. You know it's already past midnight, don't you?"

"…Midnight? …I didn't realize it was so late." After a moment's pause, Brunhild continued, "I'm too scared to sleep."

"Scared? Of what?"

What could the woman who had knocked out Sigurd in a matter of seconds possibly be scared of?

"The movie I saw with you this afternoon."

The movie… The horror movie they'd watched together?

"What's so scary about a movie like that? It's obviously fake. If anything, you're a lot scarier than ghosts," Sigurd said in a teasing tone, but her glum expression didn't change.

"It made me think about death," she said.

Sigurd waited for what she would say next.

"In that film, the dead became ghosts and wandered the earth… Is that truly what happens? Is that what awaits me after death? What if my fate is even more terrifying?"

Thinking about it that way made death seem unbearably scary.

Brunhild's eyes lowered. It seemed she was seriously frightened.

"…No one thinks that way after seeing that movie," Sigurd said, and then he sat down next to her.

The rose garden was filled with a sickly sweet scent. But there were also comforting scents mingling with it. A soft atmosphere faintly wafted around them. It was the natural scents that surrounded Brunhild, who had grown up eating the fruits of Eden.

"I've heard that the scent of roses is supposed to help you get a good night's sleep, but it doesn't seem to work for me. Just like the fruit, the flowers of this land are far inferior to those of Eden. Their sickly scent makes me want to retch."

"I see," was all Sigurd said.

The two of them were silent for a while after that. Sigurd didn't try to make conversation with Brunhild anymore. He just stayed at her side.

So Brunhild was the one to broach it.

"You're not going to return to your room and get some sleep?"

"I can't do that."

"Why not?" Brunhild said with a tilt of her head.

"Well, you're too scared to sleep, right? To be honest, I don't really understand what you're so afraid of, but still, it's my fault that you can't sleep." He had been the one to take her to the horror movie without thinking about how it might affect her.

Rather than being in the garden alone, having someone like him by her side might ease her fears. That was what Sigurd was thinking.

"Do you plan to sit with me until dawn?" she asked.

"Well, I might have to get up to answer nature's call at some point."

"…How foolish."

The corners of her lips curled up awkwardly, and Brunhild cracked a small smile. The expression was alive and honest, unlike the mask of formality she wore with the servants.

Sigurd realized—he didn't dislike this smile.

Brunhild stood up. "Thank you. I'm feeling much better. I might be able to sleep now."

"Really?" Sigurd asked, looking up at her.

"If you're worried, you may escort me to my room. I'm sure my anxieties will be put to rest if you sleep with me."

"Wha—?"

Now it was Sigurd's turn to be flustered. His face went red, and he shot to his feet. "You idiot…! Don't say that sort of thing so casually to a man! Even if we *are* siblings…"

"What's wrong?" Brunhild asked. But the boy was so flustered that he didn't notice her smile had become an impish grin.

"Well, uh… You grew up on an uninhabited island, so I'm sure you don't really get it… But a man and a woman *sleeping together* is… basically…um…"

Seeing Sigurd completely at a loss for words, Brunhild burst into laughter. She held her stomach, and there were even tears in the corners of her eyes. "My goodness, my brother is so fun to tease."

Hearing that, Sigurd finally understood. "D-damn you…! You knew what you were saying, and you said it anyway?!"

"Of course I knew. And if I may take it one step further, I also knew you'd get this worked up."

Old feelings of wanting to punch her bubbled to the surface.

But he refrained.

He much preferred her playful smile to her sorrowful expression.

"I enjoy spending time with you," she said.

"Oh, really?" he replied, but he wasn't as displeased as he put on.

"So I don't want you to get too close to me."

The boy didn't understand. "…Am I a burden to you?"

"Not at all. Considering my position and my goal, I should welcome you."

"So we're fine, then."

"Yes, but…"

A passing cloud obscured the light of the moon. After falling into thought for a while, Brunhild opened her mouth again.

"I don't know what the future holds…," she prefaced, before saying,

"…but I'm sure I'll end up hurting you. Terribly."

Silence fell once more.

Brunhild seemed to be waiting for his response. Something like, *What do you mean? What are you planning to do?*

But he didn't say anything. He wanted to, but he didn't.

His reasoning was simple.

It was an unpleasant subject.

She was returning to the forlorn girl in the rose garden.

If I press the matter, then she really won't be able to sleep again.

That worry kept Sigurd's mouth firmly shut.

The two were silent for a time, but eventually she turned away from Sigurd in resignation. From behind, her small stature looked somehow listless.

Left behind in the garden, Sigurd looked up at the night sky.

In the end, he hadn't been able to send the girl back to her room smiling.

His sigh melted into the night sky.

Finally, the day of the Typhon address arrived.

The venue was a community center in the capital. It was to be held in a large auditorium that was used for lectures from prominent figures. There was plenty of tiered seating before the podium.

The highest-ranked person there was Second Lieutenant Brunhild. At first, Colonel Sachs had also planned to attend, but when Brunhild said, "I can't be under your care forever. I'm a second lieutenant," he'd had no choice but to back down.

The large auditorium was filling up.

Ultimately, three hundred of Typhon's members populated the venue.

Some newspaper reporters pursuing Brunhild tried to get in, but they were removed by her order. She said she wanted to eliminate even the slightest elements that might agitate the members of Typhon.

The members gathered in the venue were eerily quiet. Seeing this as the calm before the storm, the soldiers who had been entrusted with the guarding of the young second lieutenant were uneasy. Though Typhon labeled themselves an environmental group, they were, in truth, a radical religious group.

Even though Brunhild had not yet arrived at the podium, the auditorium was already filled to bursting with hostility and malice toward her.

The members of Typhon perceived Brunhild Siegfried to be sacrilegious.

The dragonslaying nobility, the Siegfried family, was the greatest enemy for Typhon, who worshipped dragons. That someone of their bloodline, of all people, would call themselves the child of a dragon was beyond cursed to them.

The primary purpose of the meeting that day was to explain that Brunhild Siegfried was "*not the daughter of a dragon*"…

But from the start, Typhon never had the slightest intention of listening.

The reason Typhon had appeared at this address was very simple. It was to mentally tear down this girl who called herself the child of a dragon and make it so she would never come out in public again.

Every soldier assigned to Brunhild's personal guard was worried that things would turn violent.

As tension mounted all around them, the time came for the address to begin at last.

Second Lieutenant Brunhild Siegfried, clad in a military uniform, stood at the podium.

The members of Typhon were still quiet. But if Brunhild was to say even a word, then no matter how friendly she was toward Typhon, an all-out attack of sophistry would begin.

"…" The second lieutenant was silent.

The soldiers who guarded her thought this natural. Even Brunhild could understand that she was being exposed to a veritable sea of ire. Though she looked like an adult, on the inside, she was a sixteen-year-old child. Half the soldiers chuckled to themselves, thinking *Serves you right*, while the other half genuinely felt bad for her.

That's when it happened.

The malice that had filled the venue began to melt away.

Brunhild opened her mouth. "Thank you very much for gathering here today. I will now begin the address. I am a second lieutenant of the Norvelland army, Brunhild Siegfried. First, to give you an outline…"

The explanation that Brunhild Siegfried carried out was perfect. She was able to speak just as she had rehearsed many times beforehand.

Eventually, the ill will that Typhon held for her evaporated.

Once the explanation had concluded, the mood of the venue was 60 percent amicable toward Brunhild, while another 30 percent seemed to be confused by her. And that confusion didn't even have hostility in the last 10 percent, in particular, who streamed tears, applauded, and cheered, or even wound up putting their hands together in a praying pose.

It was the best possible result, but at the same time, such a situation could never happen.

Perfection, for this information session, wasn't possible.

Even if Brunhild had carried out the explanation just as per rehearsal, Typhon never would have been satisfied by it. They could never be applauding Brunhild when their goal was an attack on her.

But the fact was that the meeting had ended peacefully, with some so consumed by emotion that they had been whipped into a frenzy. The soldiers guarding her tilted their heads, but they were convinced that Brunhild's speech had gone well and that they were free to go.

It was the night after the Typhon address.

It happened at midnight, when the crescent moon glowed blue.

Thirty-two black dragons and ten white dragons—a total of forty-two dragons—suddenly launched a surprise attack on the city of Nibelungen.

Even if it was the capital of the Norvelland Empire, famous for their dragonslayers, nothing could have prepared them for this. No… There wasn't a single nation on the planet that was prepared for dragons to go on the offensive. Dragons had only ever been the guardians of Edens. So long as the islands were left alone, they would remain passive.

This was the first time in recorded history that dragons had amassed a group and attacked people.

The dragons that came flying in were each about five to eight meters tall. Though this classified them as midsize, their claws tore like steel through paper, and their jaws could easily crush a human's skull. Mere handguns wouldn't pierce through their hard scales.

And Commodore Sigebert, their ray of hope, was nowhere to be found. He and the Balmung were both still at sea.

The city fell into a great panic.

As people were running about trying to escape the dragons, there was a boy who faced them. It was Sigurd.

There was no way the police would be able to stop the dragons' invasion, and the army was called to deploy. However, the army was slow to respond to the unexpected situation, and they dragged their heels quite a bit until ordering the unit to move out. Sigurd had headed out to defeat the dragons on his own. He'd come to the decision that if he had sit around and wait for the order, his inaction would cost lives.

However, the outcome was not favorable.

On top of a brick arch bridge, Sigurd was facing off against a black dragon. He had acted as bait to allow a parent and child to escape imminent attack.

The sword in Sigurd's hands was broken in the middle. He was wounded, and the blood dripping from his forehead was blinding his right eye.

He was just fighting to defend himself. Defeating a dragon wasn't impossible, but it was beyond his ability. It wasn't that Sigurd was weak. Fundamentally, dragons were just that much stronger than humans. Sigurd had also been able to handle a gun, so at first, he'd been fighting the dragon with a machine gun. But even after firing every bullet in his magazine, he hadn't managed to kill even a single dragon.

The dragon he was facing off against took flight and swung its claws.

He tried defending himself with his broken sword. But the enemy was powerful, and the sword left Sigurd's hand, spinning around as it went. The claws he'd failed to block tore through the flesh of his right leg.

"—!"

Sigurd fell to his knees. He could no longer flee nor block.

"Damn you…"

The black dragon's inhuman eyes glared at Sigurd. And then it came at him again. He knew he was going to die. He would either be sliced in two by those claws, or his body would be crushed in its jaw.

But that didn't happen.

A silver shadow swept in between Sigurd and the dragon with incredible speed.

And then the black dragon froze.

After a pause, only the black dragon's head moved. It slid downward. The dragon's head had been cut off. The headless body fell a beat later with a dramatic thud.

"Are you all right?!"

The sound of the voice was bloodcurdling, but it was also a voice he'd heard before. With that, Sigurd finally realized who the silver shadow was.

"Brunhild…?"

Bearing the legendary dragon-killing sword Falchion in her hand, Brunhild stood before him.

As Sigurd was lost in his confusion, Brunhild ran up to him. "Why didn't you wait for the dispatch order?!" she screamed as she touched his face and body. She was checking the severity of his wounds.

"These wounds are significant…but not life-threatening." Brunhild looked relieved, then drew away. "Stay right where you are."

"If I were the type to say, 'understood,' then I wouldn't have come out into the city without waiting for the order…" Sigurd tried to stand up, but the wound on his right leg made him stumble.

Brunhild caught him. "It's no use trying to stand with that wound." She practically forced Sigurd to sit. "If you move around too much, you'll tear your tendon, and there's no coming back from that."

It was frustrating, but Brunhild was right. He didn't have the strength left to fight. But even if he couldn't fight, then there were things he could do as a noncombatant.

"I get that I can't fight," he said. "I'll take refuge before I'm attacked by another dragon." He had to, or this time he would certainly die.

"No, stay on this bridge. It would be worse if you went off somewhere." For some reason, Brunhild told him to stay.

"What're you talking about? We're right in the middle of a bridge. If we're attacked by a dragon, there'll be nowhere to run…"

"It'll be all right. I won't let them near you. No matter what."

That silenced Sigurd—since her words were completely unwavering. He was certain she would actually keep the dragons from coming close to the bridge. Her words were powerful enough to make him believe that.

"…Fine. I'll be here." His voice carried resignation.

So it's not just in mock combat; this is how it is, even in a real battle.

He couldn't reach Brunhild's level in any respect.

He would be lying if he said it wasn't frustrating. But at this point, he had to acknowledge it—Brunhild was the one worthy of being a dragonslayer.

So…

"Protect…"

…he decided to entrust his dream to her.

"…protect the city…protect everyone."

It sounded so pathetic he wanted to cry, but he somehow held back the tears.

Hearing that from Sigurd, Brunhild was silent for a while. After a moment's pause, she opened her mouth. "I am a daughter of the Siegfried family—and a second lieutenant."

The Falchion glittered red under the streetlights.

"I will fulfill the role demanded of me as second lieutenant."

Hearing that, Sigurd was relieved. Brunhild would see his wish fulfilled.

Sigurd quietly watched her race off.

Speaking purely in terms of results, they succeeded in repelling the dragons.

But getting there cost fifty-four dead and three hundred injured. What's more, they only managed to kill thirty-two of the forty-two dragons, and all ten of the white dragons managed to escape.

But this was much less damage than they could have taken.

Since Second Lieutenant Brunhild had, with her frenzied efforts, killed many black dragons.

Since the military's response had been stalled, and then stalled some more, her efforts had stood out.

Her silver hair opposite the dragons' black, she had looked to the people like a symbol of justice and mercy. The people who had been saved by her had called her not second lieutenant, but "dragonslayer."

The sight of Brunhild wielding the dragonslaying sword Falchion as she brought down the evil dragons had been burned into the people's eyes.

That, and the sight of her surrounded by multiple dragons being torn apart.

The people said that the white dragons had been even stronger than the black dragons.

The people said the dragonslayer had continued to fight alone and then had finally run out of strength.

No matter how powerful the dragonslaying maiden was, she was too greatly outnumbered.

They said the broken Falchion flew into the air, and a pillar of blood flew up from the girl's body. And as she fell down on her face, a white dragon bit into the flesh of her stomach.

The people's hope died then. They believed their fate had been sealed.

But that was when the main forces of the army rushed in. Finally, the dispatch order had gone out. The efforts of the dispatched soldiers saved the lives of the civilians who had been there.

After the dragons had been driven off, something resembling a filthy old rag remained.

It was Brunhild, torn to shreds, gazing into the air with unfocused eyes.

As she was carried away, a different shade of red spread through her crimson military uniform.

This was all that remained of the girl who had just minutes ago been revered as a dragonslayer.

Though she was still breathing, she was clearly beyond saving.

The newspapers all wrote stories about her.

Brunhild had been famous to begin with. Being a young and beautiful officer was already enough to make her newsworthy, but the way the reporters picked out her heroism and tragedy just made her all the more so.

The articles were a gratuitous blend of fact and fiction. They said that over one hundred dragons had attacked, and they sensationalized Second

Lieutenant Brunhild's exploits to the point where she was celebrated as much as the legend of the first Siegfried. If all the articles were true, then at the very least, Second Lieutenant Brunhild had been in three places at once and, after diving into a sea of bloody combat like some god of war, had had several different grand and heroic deaths.

No one knew what the truth was at this point. And they didn't care, either.

All that remained was the legend of the tragic dragonslayer Brunhild and fierce criticism of the military's slow response.

Brunhild had not died that day.

The publications reporting that she had perished after the fight had twisted the truth, but this was to be expected. After all, Brunhild had suffered wounds that would have absolutely killed a normal person. It was only thanks to her body, having been raised in Eden, being far more tenacious than that of humans, that she managed to survive.

When she was carried into the military's hospital, she was undoubtedly in critical condition.

The situation continued to be unpredictable. No one aside from members of the medical staff were permitted to see her.

The first visitor allowed to her side came one week after the attack—Colonel Sachs. His visitation was limited to ten minutes.

When Sachs entered the room, Brunhild was still hardly able to move. She must have been sleeping, as her eyes were closed. She was covered in bandages, and there was an IV drip in her arm. The slight bit of skin that was visible was swollen dark red.

"Brunhild…," he said, though not to her. She was such a painful sight to behold, her name had spilled out of his lips.

But the girl awoke.

Brunhild opened her eyes a sliver, slowly moving her eyeballs to look at Sachs.

"Col…onel…"

"You don't have to talk. I just came to check on you today," Sachs said in the most peaceful tone possible, as if trying to comfort her. But privately, he was in quite a panic. He didn't want her to expend any energy unnecessarily. "Don't you worry about me. I'll be leaving right away."

"You...can't... Col...onel... Wait...please." Her eyes became glossy. It seemed like it wasn't only because of her wounds that her voice was trembling.

"Was...I...not...useful...as a second...lieutenant...? Was my title... purely...decorative?"

He felt like a blunt weapon had cracked him in the back of the head.

"I...don't want to be a decoration..."

Oh, was that it?

He knew she had fought madly.

And he also knew that after all those reckless efforts, she was now here, in this state.

He had his thoughts about why she had fought until she ended up this way.

...But could it have been because he had been the one pushing her?

Now that he thought about it, even before doing the Typhon address, she had said...

"I can't have you watching over me forever. Because I'm a second lieutenant."

Because I'm a second lieutenant.

If that was the case, then he had done something unforgivable.

He had lived forty years. He understood that sometimes an offhand remark could truly hurt someone.

But he had done that very thing to her.

Just because she looked mature, and she was clever and wise beyond her years...

He thought he'd understood...

...that she was just a child.

A sixteen-year-old...

"You're not a decoration."

He would have liked to hold her hand tightly, if possible.

"You did well, Brunhild. You saved many lives. You went above and beyond the call of duty for a second lieutenant. No, what you did goes beyond rank entirely."

"Col...onel..." The line of a tear streaked from the corner of her eye to her cheek. "Col...onel... Colonel Sachs..."

"I was so scared," she admitted. "When I was surrounded by dragons... I thought...I would die. And then...my heart...started to hurt... I wonder why..."

I want to see my father.

"That's what I felt..."

Something caught in Sachs's chest.

...Ah, Sigebert.

You really made the wrong decision.

Tears welled in his eyes, even though he was too old to cry. But he held them back, willing himself not to cry in front of the girl.

The one who should be by her side is not me, but you.

"...I will do something."

It's important to protect national interest. But it's not right for me *to be the first one to come see her when she's* your *daughter.*

A nurse entered the room. Sachs's ten minutes were up.

"Brunhild... I'm going. Get some rest..."

"No..." Large teardrops fell from her eyes, as if breaking through a dam. "Don't go... Don't...go... I don't...I don't want to be alone..."

Brunhild tried to move, and the nurse, in a panic, rushed over to restrain her.

Shaking off bitter feelings, Sachs left the sickroom.

In that moment, he was firmly resolved to bring Sigebert back—the father she had been begging to see.

A week passed.

Friends and acquaintances were allowed to see Brunhild in the hospital. She had apparently recovered enough to be able to sit up on her own.

Sigurd headed to her sickroom with a small get-well-soon gift in hand.

"Come in," said a sweet voice after he had knocked on the door.

The sickroom was a private room. Brunhild looked so fragile it seemed she would be blown away as she lay on the bed. The bandages wrapped around her face and arms looked painful.

But the moment Brunhild looked at Sigurd, she said, "Oh, it's you?" and easily sat up.

"…You seem well," Sigurd groaned. He sat down on the chair left at the bedside.

"All the newspapers were really so dramatic about it. Even I didn't think they would go *that* far… Oh yes, the recent hit was *Der Flügel*. What a masterpiece of fiction. I faced a swarm of over a thousand dragons all on my own, wielding the legendary greatsword Balmung in one hand, and died once dragons finally ripped me limb from limb.

"If you want to read it, then look around on the shelf," she said with a laugh. He understood this was her own brand of humor, but he couldn't bring himself to smile at all.

If she hadn't been wounded, then he would have grabbed her by the lapels.

"…I was worried about you," he choked out. That surprised Brunhild a little.

"I was raised in an Eden, so I can endure more than the average person. Even with wounds that would kill an ordinary person, I can just barely hold on. You didn't believe those gossip magazines, did you?"

"This isn't about being able to withstand more damage."

Sigurd had regretted it, the whole time—ever since the night of the attack.

He remembered their exchange on the bridge.

Sigurd had made Brunhild take on his wish.

"…*protect the city…protect everyone…* "

When Brunhild had saved him, she had been so strong, and at that point, they hadn't known the total number of enemies, either. So he hadn't even dreamed that she would lose to the dragons.

He was so thoughtless that he was fed up with himself. If he hadn't said to protect the city, then maybe Brunhild wouldn't have gotten wounded so badly she nearly died.

"I'm glad you're okay. I really am…"

Brunhild gazed at Sigurd for a while, then said, like she was playing dumb, "Were you really worried…? About me…?"

"Don't make me say it again."

The girl lowered her eyes and said weakly, "Well… I'm sorry…"

"It's…it's not like I'm mad at you."

To cover the awkwardness, Sigurd tossed the little present. It landed on Brunhild's bed with a soft *pap*.

"What's this?"

"It's something they call field rations. Though, it's still in testing. It's the latest version of travel food used by the military. You said that everything tastes bad to you, right? So I was thinking you might appreciate food that ignores flavor altogether and only considers nutritional value."

"Oh-ho! That's a good idea." Brunhild's eyes sparkled. Her voice sounded exuberant, too. She opened the packaging with her bandaged hand. Inside were three nutritional bars.

"Can you make up for one meal's worth of nutrients with just three bars?" she asked.

"Actually, three bars will keep you going for three days."

"Fantastic!"

This was the first time Sigurd had ever seen Brunhild so happy.

"Now this is a man who understands a woman's heart."

"You're the only woman in the world who would be pleased by something like this…"

But he thought that if three nutritional bars made her this happy, it wouldn't be too much trouble to get her some more.

Think about my *feelings. I've been sitting with you every day, watching you force down your meals like you can't stand them.*

"I would say this is superior, however." Brunhild's eyes were on the nutrient IV drip. "With this, I don't have to taste anything at all."

"Being perpetually connected to an IV drip must make it ridiculously difficult to get around," he said, and she gave a thin smile.

"Indeed, it does," she agreed.

"So…what about the military?" she asked. "The doctors won't tell me a thing. They say getting worked up over anything I may hear might be detrimental to my health. And it was only in the past few days that I've been allowed to read newspapers."

"Rumors are that you're getting a special two-rank promotion."

"My, my. To think that the gossip rags would circulate even in the military," she said, lifting the corners of her lips.

But Sigurd continued in a low tone, "Well, the promotion is hearsay, so don't count on it. But you've become incredibly popular among the people, so I think you can expect a medal at the very least. If you suddenly decided to get into politics, you'd probably win an election."

Your looks would probably help a lot with popularity, too, Sigurd thought, but it was too irritating to say.

"Oh... Politician... I see..." Brunhild put a hand to her mouth and considered a while. "I'll take that into consideration. But that isn't what I wanted to ask. With this recent attack by the dragons, the weakness of the city of Nibelungen has been exposed, hasn't it? Have you heard anything about how we're planning to address that?"

"...I have."

Sigurd's rank as sergeant was low. But that aside, he also had his channel as a member of the Siegfried family. If he felt like it, he could pick up on the brass's info.

"I have heard, but..." He hesitated to say it.

Brunhild's brows knit. "But what? I think there's a need to have Commodore Sigebert stationed permanently in the city. Or..."

...That subject had, in fact, been brought up.

The people strongly wished for Commodore Sigebert, the dragonslayer, to be permanently stationed in the capital. Since the tragedy of Brunhild, they wanted him to be a symbolic emotional support. Colonel Sachs, who had a close relationship with Commodore Sigebert, had headed out to his destination to convince him. It seemed that the commodore had given him a curt response, but for whatever reason this time, the colonel was persevering quite a bit in negotiation.

But why is she so worried about that?

...There was a terribly simple answer.

She was trying to get revenge for her father.

...

Sigurd squeezed his eyes shut.

Hey, are you trying to kill Father?

He had a feeling that if he asked, she would give him an answer.

For some reason, she has no problem showing me her true feelings.

But he was scared to ask the question.

What if she responded coldly: *I am.*

What should I do?

He respected his father. He didn't want to kill him.

But he could understand Brunhild's feelings, since the parent who raised her had been killed.

He had been thinking like a victim, *I don't want my father killed...*

But the victim here was actually Brunhild.

She was living peacefully on that island before it was suddenly attacked by humans. To make matters worse, the reason they had visited the island was to secure resources. Of course she wouldn't forgive them.

So many feelings mingled inside Sigurd's head, but in terms of real time, he wasn't too worried. He gave it five seconds of thought, at most.

But Brunhild opened her mouth as if she couldn't bear to watch. "You being this kind has been my greatest miscalculation."

He pretended he couldn't hear her. He didn't ask what she meant.

He also didn't ask, *So in the end, are you trying to kill Father?*

Sigurd evaded that by asking another question. "...Hey, why do you only ever speak freely with me?"

But the answer was:

"Atonement."

With those words, he received the answer to the question he'd been avoiding.

"I'm going to kill your father."

He couldn't find the words to respond.

"You have the right to stop me."

Brunhild began to speak to Sigurd alone...

About what she had done that night—no, that day.

Chapter

3

<I have come from Eden.>

This was the first remark Brunhild had uttered at the podium during the Typhon address.

But she didn't speak the words in the official language of Norvelland.

She spoke them in the True Language.

The True Language stood at the pinnacle of all forms of communication. You could communicate anything you wanted to convey to any living creature—without moving your mouth, without making a sound.

Put another way, this meant it was also possible to communicate secret messages only to the people you wished to receive them.

This was so unexpected that the Typhon members in the hall were confused. They looked at each other, but Brunhild had continued, unbothered.

<The reports that say I am the daughter of a dragon are all true. Seeing as I am communicating with you all through the True Language, I believe you will understand.>

The existence of the True Language wasn't really known by society. But among Typhon, who worshipped dragons, it had permeated such that you could call it a fundamental part of their culture. Although they were incorrect in perceiving it as *dragon language* rather than a *universal language*, that posed no problem. In fact, given that she was calling herself a dragon's daughter, their mistake would work to her advantage. Brunhild had thoroughly researched Typhon beforehand, and she was also aware of their misunderstandings.

<The military cannot hear what I am saying. This message, I deliver only to you, devout followers—and not to your ears, but your very souls. If you doubt me, you may cover your ears. My words will still reach you.>

A number of people tried plugging their ears, as instructed. But Brunhild's words reached them all the same.

<From this moment forward, my mouth will communicate a different message than the one you are hearing in the True Language.> She touched a finger to her shapely lips. <However, this is merely a lie to deceive the eyes—rather, the ears of the foolish soldiers. My true goal aligns with yours. What I am speaking in the True Language is what I truly wish to convey.>

Brunhild's lips moved. "Thank you very much for gathering here today…"

<I know your desires. You worship dragons and seek the salvation of your souls in the Kingdom of Eternity after death… This is fact. I am a human who has been promised all that I desire in the Kingdom of Eternity once my days have come to an end. I wish the same for all of you. I wish to guide you there.>

The naked hostility that had filled the venue dispersed. At the same time, a powerful confusion rippled across the crowd.

<In the Kingdom of Eternity, there is no conflict. There is no discrimination based on race or sex. I'm sure you all already know about His land, so I will explain no further. Dragons are messengers from God in the Kingdom of Eternity. Their sacred charge is to guide the souls of the righteous to His side after death. However… God is angry. The blood of dragons, His messengers, has been spilled by the decadent.>

Brunhild made a somber expression and continued, <With a heavy heart, God struggles with the decision of whether to abandon humanity. If that happens, then all of you, the pious and sincere, will be unable

to reach the Kingdom of Eternity. That you are all able to understand the True Language, yet unable to speak it yourselves, is proof that God has already begun to pull away.>

The most devout among the crowd covered their mouths in shock.

<I have been sent to bear witness. I will judge whether humanity is worthy to be guided to the Kingdom of Eternity. If you seek entry into His hallowed land, you must first cleanse the disgrace of the dragonslayer's sins. You shall make an offering of the head of the dragonslayer.

<The name of the one who must die is Sigebert Siegfried.

<He is my blood father. To say that I could kill him without a struggle would be a lie. But if the sins amassed by my people can be cleansed with the removal of my father's head...then I will harden my heart. Even if, as a result of losing the dragonslayer, this land will be overrun by its neighbors and its people killed, so long as your hearts are pure, your souls will be saved after death. Between the momentary happiness that is human life and the eternal comfort that awaits in paradise—there is no question which is more important.>

The girl's red eyes fixed on the believers.

<I understand if there is any confusion. Some of you may be failing to follow my words, and others may not trust me. That is the obvious reaction. But even so, I beg you to have faith in me. Tonight, please come to Cannon Hill, where the moon shines brightest. There, I will prove to you that the blood of the dragon flows through my veins.>

That was the secret speech she'd given at the public venue.

Cannon Hill was the holy ground of the dragon faith from the northern region of the Norvelland Empire.

Short trees dotted the yellow ocher, wasteland-like hill. The temple that deified the dragons was not so loud and grand, but history was carved into its foundations.

Now, there was no one inside the temple except for Brunhild. Evoking her rank as second lieutenant, she had forbidden anyone else from entering. Fundamentally, a mere second lieutenant didn't have the authority to do such a thing, but civilians had no way of knowing that. Some important person from the military with a proper identification had given the order, so they had done as commanded.

By evening, Brunhild had already arrived at the cathedral.

A religious fresco was drawn on the ceiling. It was a painting of a dragon leading a great crowd of people into the heavens. With the rising dragon in the uppermost position, the humans were floating as if being pulled upward. The farther down one's eyes traveled, the darker the shades of the image became. At the very bottom, people enveloped in black flames were writhing in agony.

The dragon that was guiding people was covered in silver scales.

The title of the painting was "The Power of the Holy Dragon Lucifer." It had been painted by an artist in the Middle Ages.

I can use this, thought Brunhild.

The moment that thought crossed her mind, she felt a sharp pain in her chest, and she fell into self-loathing.

She had recalled the voice of her beloved.

<Through the fruit of knowledge, you will now be more sensitive to the subtleties of the human heart than any other. You must not use this gift to deceive others. Remember, God is watching you.>

When the sun set, people began filing into the cathedral, here and there.

They were the believers of Typhon. A few of the hastier ones came up to her, requesting that she hurry up and show them the evidence—the proof that Brunhild was the daughter of a dragon—but Brunhild held them back with the True Language.

Even once it was past time, Brunhild didn't start for a while—because she wanted as many of the followers of Typhon as possible to gather here.

It was about fifteen minutes past the promised time. The number of gathered followers was forty-two. Judging that there would be no more, Brunhild began to speak.

<First, I offer my thanks to those of you who came here with faith in me. You are the ones I trust as true allies.>

It was difficult to say that all the people who had come to the cathedral had faith in Brunhild.

There were some who had come to the temple believing that she truly was the daughter of a dragon, but not many. About half the attendees were skeptical, while most of the rest were similar to the crowd from earlier that afternoon. They had come to satisfy their curiosity or seize any opportunity to berate her.

Despite picking up on this, Brunhild kept up the appearance of trusting them as she continued. <**This afternoon, I told you all that I am the daughter of a dragon. Now you shall have your proof.**>

Brunhild rolled up the right sleeve of her military uniform and removed her glove.

She exposed an arm, covered by white scales. <**This arm is cloaked in the scales of my father.**>

Well, it wasn't as if there was nobody who accepted then that Brunhild was a dragon's daughter. But most of them were looking at her arm with dubious eyes. They had to be thinking that it was an elaborately made fake. That would be the obvious thought.

Brunhild then plucked one of the scales from her arm. A second later, a trickle of red flowed from the spot.

Brunhild licked the scale with her tongue like a snake, then handed it to a male believer who was standing nearby. He was a highly susceptible person—and a fervent believer. Tears had streamed down the young man's cheeks at the Typhon address that afternoon, and even now, he was extremely moved just from seeing her right arm.

<**Please eat my scale.**>

The believer seemed nervous, but eventually he replied, "Y-yes, ma'am!" his voice almost a shout, and tossed the scale into his mouth.

Instantly, the young man's body began to glow.

"Oh…ugh…ah…," the young man groaned.

Lumps undulated over his back, then sprouted. His shoulder blades tore through his skin and transformed into wings. Lightning coursed across his body, and his skin began to change into scales. His neck extended before their eyes, his face elongated into a snout, and his pupils lengthened vertically, like fissures. His canines enlarged and became sharp like knives.

The devoted young man had turned into a white dragon. His body was about eight meters long.

If you put a dragon's scale in your mouth, you would be temporarily transformed into a dragon. That was something that Brunhild had personally learned four years ago, when she had traveled to the Norvelland Empire.

Many of the believers were unable to move. Witnessing firsthand such an astounding situation would generally make people freeze up. After a few moments, some of the believers cried out in fear and tried to run.

<W-wait! Everyone!> the young-man-turned-dragon cried out, stopping them. His voice was not a roar, but indeed the young man's voice. It was also in the True Language.

<I'm all right! Guys! I'm not going to attack you!> The voice of the young man made the fleeing believers halt immediately.

The young man's name was Alexei. He was a particularly faithful member of Typhon, people trusted him deeply, and he had a high position in the organization. It was because they heard his voice that he was able to stop them from running.

This was the reason Brunhild had chosen him as the first to share a scale with. She had learned his position in the group from scanning the pamphlet that described the group's activities, and she'd been able to confirm his own deep faith just by looking at him.

<You feel the dragon's power, don't you?> Brunhild asked.

<Yes... I feel incredible energy radiating from my core. It feels good...>

<And you still maintain your reason and your faith?>

<Yes. My loyalty to the Divine Dragon has not changed.>

Brunhild approached Alexei and touched the scales that covered his body. And then she turned around to face the believers and called, <All of you, please try approaching him, too.>

To show that he had no hostility, Alexei bowed his head to the believers.

The believers timidly approached Alexei. By touching his scales, they were astonished by their hardness; and then touching his muscles, they were shocked by their strength.

<The scales of a dragon will repel bullets. No sword or spear can pierce them, either. And the power concealed in our flesh can blow away a tank in one swipe.>

Looking at Alexei, Brunhild said, <Please try to will yourself to return to human form.>

Alexei firmly closed his eyes, and he regained the form of a young man.

Brunhild pulled out one of her scales and held it up so everyone could see. <I wish to share this power with all of you.>

Some became a little excited. The girl's red eyes fixed on those people who showed interest and memorized them.

Brunhild thrust a finger at the ceiling. <Behold the fresco on the ceiling. Look at how pure men's hearts were—and how they perceived the truth.>

Her claw was pointed at the fresco of the white dragon guiding the people. <The fresco on this ceiling depicts us. We must transform into dragons and guide the ignorant masses. I have come from my Eden in order to grant dragon scales to those who share my goal. I wish to guide humanity to the Kingdom of Eternity. I ask that you please accept a scale, become a dragon, and fight.>

There was no one who did not want a scale.

It wasn't as if all the believers were pious, however. Some of them were plotting to use the scales for their own self-interest. Whether they were a pious believer or someone with ulterior motives couldn't be known from appearances.

Before handing out the scales, Brunhild asked two or three questions, considering them a "confirmation of faith." She did so for all the believers. The nature of the questions, as well as the people's replies, was not important.

What Brunhild was watching for was the sparkle in their eyes when replying, the tone of voice, and the movements of their fingers and facial muscles. Reading the faint signs people emitted unconsciously, Brunhild judged whether the believers before her were blind followers.

For the blind believers, she put the scale in her mouth before handing it over.

While for the schemers, she handed over a scale without putting it in her mouth.

She distributed scales to all forty-one believers, aside from Alexei.

Brunhild gave the signal, and then all the followers aside from Alexei swallowed their scales.

Just as Alexei had become a dragon, the forty-one became dragons.

The one thing that was different was that, of the forty-one, nine of them became white dragons, and the remaining thirty-two people became black dragons.

The light of intellect shone in the eyes of the white dragons, and they gazed at the black dragons in a confused manner.

All the black dragons hung their heads in subservience to Brunhild.

<Those with guilty consciences will become lesser black dragons,> Brunhild said, but this was a lie.

Black or white was decided based on whether there was any of Brunhild's saliva on the scale she handed over.

Brunhild's saliva contained traces of the fruit of knowledge. Those components would work to maintain their intellect even after becoming dragons.

But if a person swallowed a scale without saliva on it, then that person would become a black dragon, subordinate to the owner of the scale. Since they had no blessings of the fruit of knowledge, they could not maintain their intellect. The black dragons were servants who would blindly obey their master's orders.

<White dragons, your pure hearts have been chosen by God. Please think back on the conduct of those who have become black dragons. Did they not habitually engage in some behavior that spits in the face of God? Were they *truly* devout?>

It was an unfair question to ask, as no one could be a perfectly devout follower every second of every day.

But the white dragons did not notice that Brunhild's question was an unfair one. In fact, they seemed greatly convinced. All the people who would have noticed it was unfair had been made into black dragons.

Not only had they been blind believers as humans, but now they were being told they were "chosen by God." That gave the people who had become white dragons a sense of superiority that robbed them of their real intelligence.

…*Well, many of the white dragons…were young people, after all,* Brunhild thought.

There was a reason that Brunhild had not made all the believers into black dragons.

The black dragons were under Brunhild's command. However, since they were not sapient, she was unable to give them complicated instructions. If she told them to attack people, then they would do as told, but they couldn't adapt to the situation and change their decisions. They were made to keep attacking until they received a new order.

What Brunhild needed were pawns who would blindly believe in her— and who could also follow minute instructions.

For the strategy the dragon's daughter was considering then—

for the performance to be staged that night—

the restraint to stop when she was on the verge of death was important.

Brunhild finished her story. The sunlight was filtering in from the windows of her sickroom.

It took time for it to sink in. It wasn't that he hadn't understood the meaning of what she had told him—Sigurd figured it was because he didn't want to accept it.

"Then…what…?" Sigurd finally began to speak. "You're saying…you killed the people of this city?"

"That's right."

"Don't lie to me. I mean, you said… When I asked you to protect the people of this city, you agreed."

"I didn't. I only said that I would fulfill my role as second lieutenant."

"You don't think anything of it? Dragging in so many innocent people who had nothing to do with you?"

"I don't. Their lives meant nothing to me. If it would bring me closer to accomplishing my goal, I would use the same method over and over again."

"Then why did you save *me*?!" The chair fell over with a clatter. Sigurd surged to his feet and grabbed Brunhild by her lapels. "You should have let me die, too! Whether I lived or not had nothing to do with your goal! There was no reason for you to save me!"

"You're special."

Sigurd's eyes widened, and he stopped.

Special. That's what she said.

If…if Brunhild were to see him as a friend, for example…

…*then my words might reach her.*

If they were friends.

But…

"I can use you."

He could have never anticipated that she would say that.

"You are the son of my enemy. If my estimation is correct, then the one he truly cares for is not me, but you. I can think of any number of ways to use you. You could even become the sword that pierces his heart—my trump card. In terms of importance, you're even more valuable than Sachs."

That's why I saved you.

"I gave the dragons the order not to get close to the bridge where you were." She attacked Sigurd with words sharp like blades of ice. "I enjoyed spending time with you. I was able to speak my mind, and it was comfortable. I'm also at fault for having taken advantage of that. That's why I'd like to end it now."

"As I said before," the girl continued. "I'm going to end up hurting you, terribly. Well, I suppose I already have," she said, her head slightly downturned.

"Never involve yourself with me again," she finished.

The sun fell. Once it was nearly over the horizon, Sigurd opened his mouth. "I refuse."

She looked at him with sharp eyes. "Did you not understand what I just said? Human language is truly inconvenient. Fine, let me give you a what-if scenario that's easier to comprehend. If killing you were to create a situation where I could murder that man, then I would kill you without hesitation. I feel no sympathy or friendship. Since that is the only goal I have left to me—"

"You sure are stupid, for someone so smart," he said, cutting her off.

"What did you say…?"

"You feel no sympathy or friendship? Then why are you trying to push me away?"

Sigurd thought that was enough of an explanation, but the girl's brow remained furrowed.

"I'll use any tool at my disposal to kill that man," she said. "You are no exception. If there is a way to use you, then I will shed any trace of mercy and—"

"If you're explaining all that to me, you're already showing mercy. You wouldn't say something like that unless you didn't want to hurt me. You haven't realized that what you're saying is nonsensical."

Him saying all that seemed to make Brunhild finally understand. She looked startled, then trembled, as she muttered to herself. She covered her face with her hands and muttered as if she was in a delirium, "…No. That's absurd. I would…? I would…never…"

"I'm coming here again tomorrow."

She averted her eyes from Sigurd awkwardly and looked toward the window. It was right as the sun had finished setting.

"Visiting hours are over! Leave!" she spat emotionally, unable to change his mind. For the first time in her life, the girl had been outplayed.

Sigurd went to visit Brunhild the next day as well, but he was stopped by a nurse, and he wasn't able to reach the sickroom. Though the nurse was vague when explaining the reason he couldn't see her, it was quite obvious that Brunhild had made that request herself.

It was a few days after Sachs had gotten permission to see Brunhild.

In Elberg, a certain port town on the southernmost tip of the Norvelland Empire, a warship mounted with a cannon and its escort ships were moored.

Having succeeded in the conquest of another Eden one week earlier, Commodore Sigebert's ship had stopped at this port to resupply, as well as to hand over the Ashes of Eden to the army. Their original business had already concluded three days earlier.

Commodore Sigebert had been kept from leaving for the past three days—by his friend Colonel Sachs.

In a room of the warship *Fredegund*, Sachs faced Sigebert.

"This is tedious. I'm not returning to the capital," Sigebert said in a hard tone.

"But your daughter is gravely injured. You're her father!"

Sigebert's mood was the exact opposite of Sachs's indignation. When they faced off like this, it was difficult to say which of them was truly Brunhild's father.

"The girl is saying she wants to see you! Why won't you go to her?!"

"That *thing* is not my daughter."

"Enough of this…!" Sachs seemed as if he might lunge at Sigebert at any moment.

Sigebert held up a hand to restrain him. "…Listen."

Sigebert wasn't about to deny his blood relation to Brunhild. The tattoo on her wrist proved it, after all. What he wanted to say came after that. He and Brunhild had lived the past sixteen years without any interaction at all. Sigebert didn't feel any love for her, but he figured she felt the same way.

"That she thinks of me as her father and wants to see me…is beyond belief."

"There's still a bond between parent and child…that defies logic."

"…"

Sigebert fell into thought.

A bond beyond logic.

Sigebert had never felt such a thing for anyone. Not once in his entire life had he experienced a mote of tenderness for any of his friends or family members.

Sigebert saw Sachs as a friend, but that was only because of the many long years they had been in association.

Is the bond between parent and child truly so supernatural a connection?

Sigebert was skeptical about this relationship working in the positive vector, but he wasn't so hardheaded that he would reject the idea out of hand. Parents—mothers, in particular—could become stronger for their children. There were plenty of such examples.

Brunhild was a girl. He couldn't say for certain that the possibility that she felt a strong bond toward him, due to the sensitivity and strength particular to women, was zero…

But still…

"I'm not going back to the capital."

Perhaps if some other daughter had said it, he would have believed in the possibility of a bond.

The way Brunhild had glared at him in the hospital crossed his mind—the expression of deeply held resentment that had been carved there, as if she wanted to see the world burn.

There was no way that someone who could show him eyes like that would ever feel bonded with him.

"She means to kill me."

"That may well have been the case, at first. But she's changed. She's just like the girl who was raised by wolves."

But Sigebert still refused to agree.

"If you say you won't go back…," Sachs said, fists trembling in anger. "…then hear me out. You entrusted that girl to me. I'm going to be there for her."

"Do as you please. She's…all yours."

It seemed very much to Sigebert like Sachs was being taken in by Brunhild, but he didn't point that out.

Sigebert was a genius when it came to battle and military strategy, but at the same time, he was hopeless at building relationships, and he knew it, too.

If Sachs was truly being deceived by Brunhild, Sigebert figured he had no hope of using words to stand against him.

If Sachs had managed to bring her over to humanity's side, however, I would have been able to entrust the Balmung to her.

It seemed that Sigebert's plan had completely failed.

"Also…," Sachs said, "and this is setting my personal feelings aside—the civilians as well as the military big shots want you to come back to the capital, too."

"Because of the attack."

"Yeah. They killed eighty percent of the dragons that attacked the capital, but twenty percent of them got away. Everyone is scared. They're living in fear, wondering when the dragons that fled will return. The people need their dragonslayer."

"…That holds just as true for the island I mean to visit next."

They couldn't fall behind other nations in the scramble for resources.

Norvelland was poor in resources and also had meager territory. The only thing they held over other nations was their ability to kill dragons. It was by getting ahead of the other nations to secure the island Edens protected by dragons and the energy there that Norvelland could join the major powers of the world.

Sigebert returning to the capital would be of clear detriment to the nation. What's more, it didn't seem to Sigebert that putting the people of the capital at ease would necessarily be a net positive.

They didn't know when the dragons would attack, or if there even would be another assault at all. They hadn't managed to track the dragons that had fled, so they couldn't attack first, either.

"Do you plan to make me stay in the capital until the dragons attack again?" Sigebert said. "…That may take more than a month or two."

"If it were just civilians calling for it, maybe we could have made them yield. No—that's unlikely this time, too. But…"

The fear of dragons was embedded deeply into the people. And that was gradually turning to dissatisfaction toward the dragonslayer for still not returning to the capital. A special alert was on in the city in preparation for an attack, but that had just amplified the people's tension even more.

"The upper echelons of the military, politicians, and clergy all want to strengthen the city's defenses. They value their own lives, after all. Even you can't reject demands from all of them."

"…True."

Sigebert fell silent. He was silent for so long that Sachs thought he had finally convinced the man.

But.

"So…the capital just needs enough strength to repel dragons, right?"

"Yeah. That's why your strength…"

"Even if I don't return…we can give the capital the ability to drive them off."

Sigebert's small pupils fixed on Sachs. "Sachs."

"What?"

"Are you my friend?"

"Huh? Why are you asking me this now…?"

"Answer me."

"…Of course I am. You and I are friends."

"I see."

Sachs didn't understand the meaning of Sigebert's question. But being a poor communicator, Sigebert needed the confirmation for what he was about to say next.

"Because I trust you, I have a request." Sigebert closed his eyes.

After a few moments of that, he eventually opened his eyes as if he'd steeled himself. "Teach my child how to operate Balmung. That will mean…you'll learn the truth, as well. You'll learn that Balmung is not the name of a cannon or a great sword…"

Sigebert removed the pendant from his neck and handed it to Sachs.

It looked like a red teardrop-shaped ruby.

"It's shaped like a gem…but it is the key to an underground room in my estate. Balmung is there. If you make contact with it…you will naturally become able to control it. That is…if you are of my bloodline…"

"So I should bring Brunhild there?"

"No, not Brunhild. Sigurd. Under no circumstance is Brunhild to know of this."

There was an edge of accusation in Sachs's eyes as he fixed them on Sigebert, but Sigebert ignored that and continued. "Sigurd will inherit Balmung and protect the city from the dragons. I believe that is a solution you won't be able to protest."

"Well, that's true enough…"

But a wrinkle furrowed in Sigebert's brow. Then he muttered, "…Having that child inherit it was the last thing I wanted."

"…You could stand to be a bit less cruel to the child."

Even now, there was a terrible misunderstanding over which "child" was being spoken of.

"It's about time for the ship to depart. I will fulfill my mission… That's all I can do," said Sigebert.

Sachs got off the boat, gritting his teeth as he watched it go—as his friend headed out to kill dragons in search of new resources, without any thought to his daughter.

The dragon's daughter recovered more quickly than a human.

One month after her hospitalization, she was allowed to be discharged.

It had been anticipated that when Brunhild was discharged, the journalists would descend upon her. So the time of her discharge was kept secret, and when she left the hospital, she used the back gate of the building. They went through the same process as the time she had been discharged from her first stay at the military hospital.

But despite that, this time, for some reason, reporters knew precisely when she was to be discharged and were waiting at the spot at the back gate. It could only be assumed that someone within the hospital had leaked information to the reporters.

At the back gate, Brunhild was surrounded by tons of reporters and showered with questions, one after another.

The servants of the Siegfried household tried to protect her, but Brunhild held them back, and she answered their questions with a smile.

"I only did what I had to, as second lieutenant," "I did nothing worthy of praise," "It's the duty of a soldier to protect civilians," "It's only natural that a member of the Siegfried family would do such a thing."

They were all perfect answers as a soldier—and as a refined lady of the Siegfried household.

Because they were all such model answers, they were boring to the reporters.

So one reporter asked a more intrusive question. "Weren't you scared of the dragons?"

There it is, the daughter of the dragon thought.

So she deliberately acted like she didn't know what to say, after having answered so smoothly until then.

The reporters sensed the response they were looking for.

After her moment of silence, the girl replied, "I wasn't scared" more quietly than before.

Then the reporters' questions came like an avalanche.

"Were you truly not scared?" "You didn't find your abilities lacking, as the dragonslayer?" "Wouldn't the real dragonslayer have been able to prevent more damage?" "What is your opinion of your father?" "Did the thought *If only my father were here* ever cross your mind?"

To all these, and similar questions, Brunhild answered with a single remark.

With trembling shoulders, she covered her face with her hands and said, "I'm sorry."

She knew well just how much meaning the reporters would choose to extract from that "*I'm sorry.*"

As the dragon's daughter was pretending to be sorrowful, a nostalgic voice rose in her mind.

< *It's not a sin to eat the fruit of knowledge. The sin lies in using the knowledge granted by the fruit for treachery, such as deceiving and tricking another.*>

In that moment, the girl's sorrow became genuine.

THE DRAGON-KILLING GODDESS MIRACULOUSLY RETURNS ALIVE!

THE TRUTH BEHIND HER TEARS!

DEEP DOWN, THE DRAGONSLAYER IS JUST A GIRL

SUCH TRAGIC DETERMINATION, IN PLACE OF HER ABSENT FATHER!

NOBLE DAUGHTER; COLD, ABANDONING FATHER

The exaggerated headlines came one after another.

Normally, there might have been pressure from the military, but there was none of that this time. The army colonel who thought of Brunhild as his own daughter had given permission for the reporting.

The tears Brunhild had cried...

There was only one person in the city of Nibelungen who knew the real reason for them.

Sigurd Siegfried.

Reading the newspaper during breakfast made him feel lightheaded. He was not Brunhild, but that day, his bread tasted like sand in his mouth.

Frankly speaking, Sigurd didn't know what to do. He had gone to the hospital every day, but he had been driven away each time. Though Brunhild had returned to the estate the day before, the door to her room was locked, and he couldn't get in. Even during lunchtime, when it had usually been left open, it was still locked.

I have to stop her.

Sigurd saw Brunhild as his first-ever friend. Since he was quick to anger, people typically kept their distance from him. He just had hangers-on who latched on to him because of his family name.

Brunhild was trying to kill their father. She had reasons that made sense for her to try to do that. But he didn't want his father to be killed.

He wanted to make Brunhild give up on her revenge, if he could. He was no longer jealous that she'd gotten a high position as an elite commissioned officer, and even if she became dragonslayer after his father, he wouldn't be envious. So while he wouldn't go so far as to ask her to…reconcile with their father, he wanted her to stop trying to kill him.

And if Brunhild fumbled her murder plan, then their father would court-martial her and have her executed.

I want them both to live…

This was the seventeen-year-old Sigurd's most fervent wish.

But since he was no more than a seventeen-year-old boy, he had no way of resolving things. No—his age surely had nothing to do with it.

No matter how I think about it, this isn't something that can be resolved with words.

The flames of revenge that burned within Brunhild were fierce.

They were clearly not so weak that Sigurd could stop her. She had already dragged many people into her plans and killed them for the sake of her goal. Brunhild's assault had left fifty-four dead and as many as three hundred injured. And what's more, she herself had been included among those injured. If she was going to push herself right to the verge of death in order to fulfill her goal, then at the very least, Sigurd couldn't think of anything to say that would persuade her.

As he was worrying about this, morning came to an end. When his eyes shifted to the clock on the wall, the hands read three PM.

Someone was knocking on the door to Sigurd's room.

He tensed, thinking, *Oh! Is it Brunhild?* But this knocking was different. She would knock on the door in a reserved manner, but this knock felt vigorous.

"Come in."

The one to come in was Colonel Sachs.

Sergeant Sigurd stood up out of his seat, straightening his posture as he saluted.

"At ease. Today…isn't that sort of day."

But Sigurd didn't relax his posture.

Sachs closed the door. "Your father asked me a favor."

Sachs pulled the ruby pendant out from his pocket.

That evening, Sigurd headed for Brunhild's room. He tried to open her door without knocking. It was locked, but he pried it open with the *power* he had just acquired.

Brunhild was in the middle of finishing her lunch, a bitter expression on her face.

She looked at Sigurd in surprise. But she quickly put on a harsh expression. "I thought I told you to never involve yourself with me again…"

Sigurd didn't listen, striding briskly up to her.

He looked down at her, sitting in her chair. As if intimidating her.

She looked up at Sigurd with red eyes.

"I've acquired Balmung," he said in a strong tone. "Father decided to make me the official heir. Not you, *me*."

I've become the dragonslayer.

"Commodore Sigebert should be in a distant port. How did you confirm that he wanted you to be the heir?"

"Colonel Sachs delivered the news."

"I see." Brunhild smiled. "Isn't that nice? So your dream to be acknowledged by him has come true. I envy that. I've never once been acknowledged…"

There was no hostility in her voice at all, and it sounded lonely.

For a moment, Sigurd just about had the wind knocked out of his sails.

But he continued saying, "I've become stronger than you," in the scariest voice he could make—as if threatening her.

"Balmung isn't what you think. It's far more powerful than you can imagine. With a weapon like that in my control, you have no hope of beating me."

"If you told me what that Balmung really is, it would make my plans a lot easier to carry out, though."

"That's why I'm not going to tell you." He finally had the upper hand, and he wasn't about to let that go. "I'll be clear. So long as I have Balmung, you cannot defeat Father or me. This isn't some idle threat, so…"

…*Stop trying to kill Father.*

His voice, which had been overbearing until this point, became as feeble as if he were pleading. "I won't be so flippant as to say I understand…just what sort of pain you've gone through. I probably can't even begin to imagine. But stop this. I don't want you or Father to die. I don't want to watch you doing any more horrible things, either. Just because terrible things happened to you, and you want to get revenge…that doesn't make it okay to involve more people and get them killed."

He didn't want to say it, but he had to. "With…with the passage of time…I'm sure…even you…" But he couldn't finish the statement, after all.

So Brunhild picked it up from there. "Yes. I will heal with time."

She put a hand on the buttons of the military uniform she wore.

One after another, the buttons popped open.

She pulled her arm from the right sleeve of her uniform coat.

Underneath her military uniform, she wore a sleeveless silk camisole. So her right arm was completely exposed from the shoulder.

Her right arm was covered in silver scales.

As Sigurd turned his face away, Brunhild said, "Have a proper look, Sigurd."

"…I don't have to look to know. Your right arm is…"

"That's not what I mean. Look closely."

Sigurd timidly lifted his head.

With her left index finger, Brunhild pointed to the base of her right arm. "The scales extended this far before."

She slid her index finger up to her right elbow. "In half a year, it wound up healing this far."

The scales that had once covered up to her shoulder now only went to her elbow.

"Human healing abilities are amazing," the girl said with an ironic smile.

"When I spoke with that man in the hospital, I made up my mind. I vowed that I would get revenge for my father with this right hand, with my father's hand. I'm running out of time. I will kill him before my scales are lost."

She even saw her father in her scars.

Sigurd's gaze swam around as he wondered if there was something that could convince Brunhild.

He happened to notice a certain book tucked into the bookshelf. It was quite conspicuous among the difficult tomes there.

It was a book about a girl raised by wolves.

Brunhild also noticed what Sigurd was looking at.

Noticing that picture book, Sigurd was a little relieved.

It was a story that anyone from the Norvelland Empire would know.

The girl raised by wolves was taken in by a hunter and came to the human world. At first, the wolf girl was bewildered, but after many twists and turns, she became friendly with humans and achieved a happy ending.

If she has this book, then that means...

That had to mean that in the depths of her heart, she wished to become happy like the wolf girl.

She only tells her true feelings to me.

At first, he'd found her to be disagreeable, but she laughed like anyone else, and she would tell jokes, even if they weren't funny. She could be surprisingly timid, and she was the kind of eccentric who'd be overjoyed by rations. She spoke in an arrogant manner... But lately, he'd come to understand that she could be cute sometimes, too.

Someone like that shouldn't be okay with murder...even if it was out of revenge for her father. Surely, she didn't actually *want* to kill anyone. She had gotten those civilians involved in the assault because that had been the only way. If it were possible, she would have wished for a way to achieve her goal without casualties.

"I see, Sigurd. So *that's* how you interpreted that story."

As usual, she spoke as if she could read his mind.

"That's the right way to interpret it…if you're a human. That's what the writer meant when they wrote it. But you know what? When I read that book, I cried. I cried for the first time since coming to the lands of men."

I cried because I was scared.

"In time, the girl raised by wolves forgot her parents, who had been shot and killed by the hunter, and became human again. That book taught me that no matter how strong your feelings are, you can't avoid them fading and crumbling."

Brunhild had read the book from an altogether different point of view than a human would have.

"I decided I would never read it again, but I keep it in the room as a warning to myself. It has only been six months since I came to this land… but I can no longer remember… Even in the darkness when I close my eyes, when I try to picture my father, it's…hazy."

I'm the same way—and that's true for everyone else, too, Sigurd thought.

Surely, if told to picture their father's face, no one would be able to accurately name every minute detail.

But even if he were to say that, he doubted he could change her conviction.

Even if the same conditions applied to each of them being able to perfectly recall their fathers' faces, the connotations were completely different.

There wasn't a single person with the verbal chops to talk her down anyway, Sigurd figured. She was frighteningly quick-witted.

So there was nothing to do but show her with force.

"I won't let you kill Father. But I won't kill you. I could if I wanted to, but I never will. I'll beat you within an inch of your life if I have to.

But don't make me do that. Just don't," Sigurd spat, and then he left the room.

As he left the room, there was a ration clasped in his hand.

If Brunhild had been frightened by any of my threats...I was going to give this to her as an apology.

He was gripping the ration case so tightly it hurt.

The girl's crimson eyes hadn't wavered even slightly. The flames burned intensely with his every word.

That night it rained. The gentle drizzle soaked the sidewalk.

Sachs was reading a book in his study. The hands of the clock were already pointing to a time it was fair to call the small hours. Right as he was thinking about going to sleep, the butler came.

He said there was someone standing in front of the estate with no umbrella.

Sachs ordered the butler to immediately drive away such a suspicious person, but the butler's face clouded as he said, "But...it looks like the one in front of the estate is the young lady of the Siegfried family."

Sachs dismissed the butler and headed to the door himself.

When he opened the door, Brunhild was standing there. She had no umbrella, and her red military uniform was soaked. Her face was also soaked with a liquid that was not rain.

"Wh-what happened...?!"

Coming to my house at this hour with your face like that—just what on earth happened?

The girl just sobbed, her face red.

"Come inside. You'll catch a cold."

While Brunhild was warming herself up in the shower, Sachs prepared some hot milk himself. *Perhaps I should have hired a maid instead of a butler*, he thought. He didn't know what he would do once she was finished with her shower. He didn't even have any clothes to put on her. Having distanced himself from women at age twenty-four, Sachs obviously had no women's clothing available.

Left with no choice, he laid out his own unfashionable sleeping attire. There was nothing else he could do.

A while later, Brunhild came to Sachs's room.

Brunhild wore only the top of the sleeping attire. She wasn't wearing pants. Since Sachs's sleeping attire was too big for her, the top looked like a baggy dress on her. Her pale knees were on full display.

"And the pants…?" he asked.

"…I'm sorry. I know you went to the trouble of laying them out for me… But um, they were too big… The elastic was loose…"

Well, of course. He just hadn't noticed. Taking into account the difference between Brunhild's slim waist and his own, this outcome wasn't much of a surprise.

"Damn… Just about all the clothing here will be a poor fit for you…"

"It's all right. Look, please." Brunhild spun around. The water droplets that wet her hair sparkled as they scattered. On her, even unfashionable menswear transformed into a lovely dress.

After spinning around, she smiled softly. To Sachs's eyes, she looked like a goddess of flowers.

"See, it's fine," she said.

"…Mm." His face broke into a smile on its own.

When they'd first met, he'd thought of her as an uncanny girl.

The way her dark-red eyes had seemed to be observing him had been creepy.

But now she would show him expressions like this.

"Besides, your clothing smells kind of nostalgic. It puts me at ease."

"…Nostalgic?"

"It reminds me of when I was in Eden…when the father who raised me was still alive…," Brunhild trailed off.

Could it be that this child thinks of me as…?

For a second, a certain thought crossed Sachs's mind, but he quickly shook it off. He judged coldly that such a thought was clearly too convenient for him.

"I warmed up some milk. It might calm you down." Sachs slid the milk toward her and asked, "So…what's the matter, at this hour? Did something happen?"

Brunhild held the cup in both hands. It was such a squirrel-like gesture. She gazed at the steam rising off the milk, not making to take a sip. "Oh no, it's nothing. I just happened to be in the area."

"That's obviously not the case." He had witnessed her standing there out in the rain. "You were crying, weren't you?"

It seemed she couldn't argue.

"Won't you tell me what's wrong? I might be able to help."

But Brunhild remained silent.

Sachs was sure of his ability to read people's faces. It was a technique backed by many years of experience. And Brunhild's expression now was that of someone who didn't want to cause trouble for others.

"We spoke before, in the hospital, didn't we?" Sachs continued gently. He wanted Brunhild to be at ease. "You asked me if it was all right to rely on me. And I answered, 'Of course it is.' My feelings haven't changed. It's no trouble at all. I want you to rely on me."

The girl finally lifted her face, and then "Colonel…" spilled from her lips. "Why is it…that when I'm with you, I feel as though I've been reduced to a child again?"

"Because you *are* still a child. Now then, what's the problem? You can tell me."

The girl still seemed to hesitate, but eventually, she began to speak, albeit with much trepidation. "I heard that Sergeant Sigurd…has become the dragonslayer. That he's been acknowledged as Commodore Sigebert's official heir."

Sachs was struck by a tightness around his chest.

"It's fine. It's only natural. After all, my elder brother has been living with our father for much longer than I have. And besides…I'm a woman," Brunhild said with a smile, but her smile was soul-crushing.

Sachs found it unbearable to look at.

"I'm…I'm a fool, aren't I? I was so naive. Since I was given the rank of second lieutenant…I may have gotten my hopes up… I thought that if I worked hard…maybe…even I…could…"

Though I already knew it, the girl said, covering her face. "It was painful to be at the estate…and before I knew it…I was in front of your place…"

It seemed as if she couldn't continue any further.

She didn't have to continue for Sachs to pick up on what she was thinking. "You really have put in so much effort. Everyone in this country knows that." Sachs came up to Brunhild's side and gently laid a hand on her shoulder.

"Colonel… Colonel…"

He was fed up with his own behavior.

He was frustrated with himself for only being able to speak in platitudes.

He hated himself for being unable to go further and be of help to her.

If—if I could…

"I wish…," the girl said with a sob. "I wish…*you* were my father."

He couldn't stand it any longer.

Sachs threw his arms around her shoulders.

I remember the winter when I was twenty-four…

The night I was stabbed by a woman.

Back then, I was a terrible womanizer. I remember telling Sigebert about just how many women I'd had, as if it were some sort of heroic exploit.

One of the women I'd fooled around with had come to tell me she was pregnant with a baby girl.

In that moment, I felt like electricity had run through my body.

A child… A girl.

It hadn't felt real.

I, myself, was still a kid…and a kid like me was going to be a father? Truly?

I still find it shocking, even now. *"Huh? Do people change in an instant like that?"*

Since that moment, I cut off all my relations with women—aside from the woman who was to be my wife.

I remember it well.

I was happy.

I was so happy.

I don't know the reason why. If forced, maybe I could say it was because

I'd finally had direction in life. My life had been nothing but taking women, eating food, getting older, and dying… And then all of a sudden, I had a clear goal. I think that's what it was.

It was light.

That child was my light—*our* light.

I think I got carried away and splurged on educational toys and clothes and dolls and stuffed animals and the like. My wife-to-be laughed at me, but I didn't mind. It had been the most meaningful use for my money to date.

Even though I still had yet to see my daughter's face, I imagined what she'd look like when she was older.

If she resembled her mother, then she would be a cute girl. If that was the case, I didn't want to let her into the army. There would've been men like me there. She would surely be a pure and innocent child, and they would try to take advantage of her. As her father, I had to protect her… But for how long? Well, if I could, I'd like to protect her forever—until I became an old man and died. But that's no good, huh? Just because she's my daughter doesn't mean she's my possession. Once she came to choose a proper man, I'd have to let her leave the nest. But, ah, I was still worried. If my child had been a boy instead, would I have had to worry nearly as much?

While Sigebert was a little fed up with me, he listened to my ramblings. "*Lately…you always talk about the same thing…,*" he said, but he always listened to the whole thing. He even said something silly like, "I bet babies are…quite warm."

Only my wife-to-be kept up with my musings, on the same level. We would talk about the same thing until day turned to night. It was so strange… No matter how many times we talked about it over and over, we didn't get even the slightest bit sick of it. I can say for certain that time was the happiest period of my life.

But there is a God.

Because if you do wrong, then judgment falls upon you.

It was on the way back from the hospital, where we'd gone for a routine health check of our unborn baby. The snow was falling silently, and it was cold. I was leaning close to the woman who would be my wife as we walked so she wouldn't catch a chill, while watching out for the icy places here and there on the road.

…Though it may not seem it, I'm a military man, so I was able to sense a sort of hostility.

But while I could sense it, there's no point if you don't have the ability to prevent it.

All too late, I realized the woman had a dagger in her hand and was dangerously close to my fiancée.

It was a woman I had dumped after a brief tryst.

I felt that if she was going to stab someone, I wanted it to be me and not my fiancée.

But the woman with the knife was never after me—she was trying to attack my wife-to-be. I didn't have the time to cut between them.

But that isn't even an excuse.

When I tried to cover her, my elbow knocked my fiancée aside.

Though I was stabbed in the stomach, thanks to the adrenaline rush, I was able to restrain the woman.

I knocked the assailant to the ground and then said, so foolishly, to my fiancée, "Are you all right?"

I killed her.

I didn't accidentally hit her in a bad spot, or anything like that.

If I hadn't thrust my fiancée aside then,

or if I had been strong like Sigebert, and I had been able to deal with the knife with more skill,

and most of all,

if I hadn't been such a womanizer,

then my fiancée wouldn't have been attacked,

and she wouldn't have landed on her belly when she fell, hard, onto the frozen street.

That day, I learned what the end of the world was.

It was something terribly plain—and painless.

Blood seeped out from her skirt and spread out on the road. The blood grew colder and colder. It seemed like the cold air was stealing away the life and warmth of that child, and I wailed, "Stop... No more..." That's about as far as I remember clearly.

If that child had survived... If she'd had a chance at birth...
If I hadn't killed her...

Then she would have been sixteen this year.
She would be the same age as the second lieutenant in my arms.

Before I knew it, I was crying. Wailing and wailing, like a little kid.

Brunhild had already stopped crying, with my arms around her as she kindly rubbed my back. Like this, you wouldn't know which was the adult.

She said quietly, "I'm not your real daughter..."

But even so...

...I won't leave your side, Father.

"This time, please rely on me."

Brunhild continued to stroke my back. Just as if she were comforting a child.

...

Sigebert...why...?

Why are you so cruel to such a good girl?

Even though you have such a lovely daughter, why do you treat her with such disdain...?

I'm so envious of you right now... It's taking everything not to hate you.

This is the girl who wants to be acknowledged by you so badly... To that end, she fought until she nearly died.

Why won't you acknowledge her inheritance?

Why won't you hand over Balmung to her?

I can't do anything for her. I'm not useful in the slightest.

But this girl says she will be with me. She tells me to rely on her.

It doesn't matter what she asks... If I could just help this girl in any way...

I suddenly happened to recall the safe in my quarters.

Stored within was the pendant Sigebert had entrusted to me.

Ah, I see.

If I wanted to, I could just give it to her…couldn't I?

I could give her Balmung.

"Brunhil…"

She stared at me blankly.

"There's something I want to give you."

What sort of look would she give me when she heard my next words? Even just imagining it put hope in my heart.

This is not a mistake.

She was much more capable than Sigurd, and she had produced results. Once it was over, that old Sigebert would understand anyway. He would understand that he should have given Balmung to her in the first place.

Giving Balmung to Brunhild was not a mistake…

"*Sachs.*"

That was when it suddenly popped up in my mind.

"*Are you my friend?*"

It was my friend's terribly curt confirmation.

I don't know why that was what made the fever that raged so violently through my head settle down.

…I confess.

I was seeing my own unborn child in Brunhild. I loved her very much. I could do anything for her sake.

But greater than that…

…was my feeling that I could not betray my hardheaded friend.

I was free to see my daughter in Brunhild.

"…Sorry."

But Brunhild wasn't my daughter, after all.

"I want you to forget what I just said."

Why was it?

That moment…for just one moment.

Brunhild looked like a completely different creature.

*   *   *

And then, I got the feeling that she looked at me with intense disappointment.

It was quite hard.

But I couldn't give it to her. Absolutely not.

"It's fine." Brunhild smiled. "Don't force yourself, Colonel. If you say so, then I'll forget all about it." With a smile, Brunhild went back to being the girl I knew so well.

That's why I was also able to get my smile back.

"I think I will take my leave soon. I can't bother you any more than I already have."

"You haven't bothered me at all."

"Really? So then may I come visit again?"

"Of course. But not while I'm working."

Brunhild clapped her hands together in joy. "Wonderful. In that case, may I please use your house as my refuge for a little while?"

"Your refuge?"

"Yes, since my elder brother comes to boast to me about how he's acquired Balmung. If I could at least learn what Balmung is, then I could find some way to retort." Eyes downcast, the girl scratched her cheek.

…Sigebert. Surely that much is no problem, is it?

I won't hand over Balmung to the girl. The appointment of dragonslayer is your decision.

But it's fine to tell her what Balmung is, isn't it? She's also a daughter of the Siegfried clan.

Besides, even if she knew the true nature of Balmung, she wouldn't be able to handle it without touching its main body. Of course, knowing what it really is does not mean becoming the dragonslayer. If you could become a dragonslayer just from knowing what it was, then I would already be one.

It's fine just to tell her this much, isn't it?

Sachs put his index finger to his lips.

"Listen. You must absolutely never tell anyone. He'd get angry at me later."

"Are you going to tell me?"

"You have the right to know what it is, too."

The girl's eyes were sparkling.

"Balmung is a fragment of God's power."

"God's...power?"

"Um, even if I tell you, you might not believe me," Sachs said as he scratched the end of his nose.

Brunhild leaned forward, saying "I'll believe anything you say."

Hmm, very cute. But I'm a little worried that kind of innocence might lead to you being taken in by a bad man one day.

"You know that before the human world was made, the universe just had God and His angels, right?"

"Of course. I've made sure to study my history."

"And that one-third of the angels became dragons and plotted rebellion against God?"

"Yes, and their leader was the first dragon, Lucifer. The evil dragon Lucifer was defeated by God and fell to hell."

"The evil dragon Lucifer was defeated by God's lightning. A fragment of that lightning remained on earth. That is the true nature of Balmung."

Brunhild put a hand to her mouth. She seemed lost in thought.

...Perhaps the explanation was a little difficult.

"When I saw Balmung's main body, it was a ball of light. It was like... a super-compressed high-energy body. But it's apparently such a powerful energy body that if a normal person was to touch it, they would be driven mad. It is a portion of God's power, after all. A human being can't hope to understand God. But humans never stopped trying to claim the power of Balmung. They went through generations and generations of research on improving the bloodline so as to give birth to a human who could control it. This was what resulted in the blood of the Siegfried clan. Only they can avoid madness when taking in God's power... No, strictly speaking, even those with the blood of the Siegfried family will go mad if they try to use God's power. But what they *can* do is accurately measure the amount they can use without losing their minds."

Sachs had also been told that Sigebert spoke so slowly because Balmung had caused abnormalities in the speech center of his brain. ...*He always did avoid talking about the important things. I've decided to stop teasing him for the way he talks.* What's more, when taken into the body, though it was slow, apparently Balmung would definitely eat away at the other functions of the brain.

"…So that's what it is?" the girl muttered. "Balmung is the power that first killed the dragons. Its origin means it was granted a dragonslaying attribute. So then the issue is how much of the power is being wielded. Even a small fraction of Balmung can no doubt render a dragon helpless. And that's how the dragonslayers got their name…"

"…Brunhild?"

"…That's what you're saying, right? Was my understanding incorrect?"

"Oh, no. I'm just always so surprised by how quick on the uptake you are. That's exactly right. Balmung will never lose to any dragon."

Brunhild laid her right hand over her left. "No creature categorized as a dragon can ever win against Balmung, is that right?"

"Uh-huh. I'm sure simply touching Balmung would hurt them quite a bit."

"…I now understand why Father did not want me to inherit Balmung." Brunhild's eyes were on her gloved hand. The hand wearing that glove was covered in silver dragon scales. "My body is half dragon. Surely I would have no hope of controlling Balmung."

"Well… We don't know that…"

He felt he had to say something to console her, but it seemed that wouldn't be necessary. Brunhild's expression was peaceful.

"I'm relieved. It's not that he didn't want me to inherit Balmung, but rather that he couldn't… Whatever the truth is, I'm thankful even for the possibility."

"…Your father does acknowledge you, Brunhild."

That part may have been a white lie, though…

"Besides…there's *another* Balmung that I can give you. Though it's not quite the one you want."

"Huh?"

"It has been decided confidentially that you will be given the Silver Honor of Balmung. Since you protected the capital from dragons."

The Silver Honor of Balmung was medal given for excellent service in battle. Brunhild was plenty qualified for it.

"Which reminds me, I heard that I might be promoted two ranks."

"Ah-ha-ha, it's clearly too early for that." Though with this girl, her becoming captain wasn't such a distant future.

"Yes, of course. I am glad for the medal, though."

"You can look forward to the conferment ceremony. There are plans to make it into something of a festival."

Brunhild's medal conferment was going to be a little different from the traditional ceremonies.

To the public, Brunhild was a tragic dragonslayer.

To give her no medal of honor at all would be setting a bad example for the military. The goal of Brunhild's conferment ceremony was to show that they did hold her in high esteem—and to bring the energy lost by the dragon's assault back to the town. Therefore, her conferment ceremony was to be held in Nibelungen Square—and open to the public.

"They're calling a military band, and they're going to make it a big celebration."

"Oh, I'm looking forward to it," she said with a smile. "Will it be the prime minister who pins the medal on my chest?"

"That's right," Sachs said, then understood what she wanted to say. "You want it to be conferred by Sigebert?"

Brunhild didn't say anything, but her silence had to be a yes.

"…I think that can be arranged."

Brunhild's expression visibly brightened. What an openhearted girl.

"We have enough material to convince the higher-ups."

The people's distrust toward Sigebert was mounting, as he was making no effort to return to the capital, despite no one knowing when the capital might be attacked by dragons. Even just one public appearance would ease the criticism toward him.

Besides, having a father confer an order to his daughter made it a more emotional story. Sachs wanted a heartwarming event like that making headlines in the newspapers.

No matter how busy Sigebert was, it was impossible for him to not have the time to come back to the capital for a day—no, half a day.

This time, Sachs wouldn't let him say it couldn't be done.

Sigurd also heard about Brunhild being given an honor. That part was fine.

The problem was how the honor would be conferred.

The medal was apparently to be directly offered from Commodore Sigebert's hand to Second Lieutenant Brunhild's chest.

If Brunhild is going to kill Father, then that's the moment.

There was one week until the conferment ceremony.

Sigurd was in Brunhild's room. Brunhild had apparently stopped trying to lock the door to rebuff Sigurd. She must have figured he'd break the lock with God's power anyway.

It was lunchtime. The two of them were the only ones in the room, and Brunhild was silently eating her lunch.

"You instigated this," he blamed her.

"I did," she replied readily.

He could have asked her what she was going to do, but there was no point in forcing her to answer.

She's frighteningly quick-witted.

Even if Sigurd learned her plans, she would certainly come up with some new plans taking his knowledge into account. Sigurd wasn't smart enough to be able to deal with that. So then it was the same as knowing nothing at all.

"Just don't try anything stupid. You can't beat Father."

"…Hey, Sigurd. It's always bothered me… Why haven't you told anyone about the fact that I want to kill him? It would make things so much harder for me if the people around Sigebert were to know of my rebellion."

"You're the perfect daughter, while I'm the unlikeable son. No one would believe a word out of me. And even if they did… Wouldn't that put you in a really terrible position?"

"I would be executed for treason."

You even know it yourself.

"…I'm begging you: Stop this."

Sigurd couldn't bring himself to say anything trite, like *Nothing comes from revenge* or *Your dead father wouldn't want this.*

So he pleaded—though he didn't have the strength to stop her.

"I can't tell you what it really is, but Balmung is something you could never hope to oppose. I'm sure…you're thinking that Father will be defenseless during the conferment ceremony. You must be planning to take advantage of that opening to go after him… But you don't get it. Father has no openings."

"You have the power of God, don't you?"

He was shocked. "Wha—? How did you know…?"

"The colonel sang like a bird. Don't blame it, though. That pitiful creature couldn't hope to offer much resistance."

"Did you…acquire Balmung?"

"I wish. It wouldn't give Balmung to me. I played the role of doting daughter to perfection… I don't understand it. It seems I lost to something… There must have been some hidden side to it that I had not yet seen.

"Although," Brunhild continued. "Even if it had given Balmung to me, there is a chance I would have not been able to use it."

Brunhild tapped on the back of her right hand with her shapely nails. It made a hard ticking sound. "The power of God is the power to destroy dragons. It's like multiplying by zero. With my half-dragon body, I would be unable to use it, and if I was struck by its lightning, there is a very real possibility that I would perish. This, I won't know about without investigating the article itself. But it's not as if I can get close to the article in question."

He felt eyes on him. Sigurd looked to see that Brunhild was watching him. When he noticed her gaze, she immediately averted her eyes.

"If it was just a small fragment of it…then I might be able to find a way out of this situation. If I had a…slightly better plan…or possibly…" After going that far, Brunhild trailed off.

Sigurd looked into her red eyes. There was no sign of calculation, or pleading, or coercion in them.

There were only feelings of weakness, as if she were seeking help.

The desire to help welled up in him, but that was out of the question. He averted his eyes.

"...Frankly, I'm stuck."

This was the first time he'd ever heard Brunhild complain. She was clenching her gloved right hand. "I decided that on the day I killed him, I would crush him with this right hand."

He felt her frustration in those words. For the killer of her father to be someone she had no hope of killing...it had to be painful.

"I'm going to be at the ceremony, too," said Sigurd. "Though I'll be in the audience...I'll be keeping watch. The whole time."

"Don't come...," Brunhild said, sounding frightened.

Though I know...that I'm one of the reasons she's got that look on her face. But what the hell else can I do?

What else can I do aside from stopping her?

"...Do you hate me?"

Brunhild's red eyes looked at Sigurd.

"You're...special."

It was the same thing that she'd said once before, at the hospital.

But it was fair to say that the secret warmth in her words now was the complete opposite of her iciness then.

"You're human... But you're a good person. To think that there are good humans in the world. There are actually kind people..."

I like you.

She sounded like she was practically in tears.

Sigurd stole away the plate that had Brunhild's lunch on it and greedily devoured the food.

After he had finished everything, he returned the plate to Brunhild.

"I won't mince words with you. It's awful to have feelings and memories of a loved one fade. And I think that as long as you're alive, there's going to be more suffering. But when that happens, I'll eat a portion of your suffering. Don't suffer the terrible taste all by yourself. Call out for me. I... I'm human, and I'm a dragonslayer, but I'm..."

He wanted to say, *I'm on your side.*

But he swallowed the words.

If I really were on her side, then I'd have to help her out and kill Dad, or it'd be a lie.

"…I'm your friend."

There was an airy sound. It was the sound of Brunhild sucking in a breath with a startled expression.

She was looking at Sigurd, teary-eyed.

"I'm sorry."

Brunhild turned her face away from Sigurd. She was looking out the window, staring at nothing.

"Let me be alone."

Her small shoulders were trembling.

Sigurd Siegfried spent the next five days in deep thought…

About whether Brunhild had given up on her desire to murder their father.

She'd cried when he'd declared he was her friend. That had to mean she'd given up on her foolish ideas.

Again and again, he made up a rationale. He believed only the information he wanted to believe, and he tried to convince himself that she had given up on her revenge. But the more layers of belief he painted on, the more he found himself realizing…he was clearly thinking that way because he knew he'd failed to change her treasonous intent.

The day he finally made up his mind was a holiday.

It had been five days since he had been chased out of her room by her small, trembling back.

There were only two days left until the conferment ceremony.

Sigurd headed to Brunhild's room. Unusually, it was not during a mealtime.

When Sigurd entered her room, Brunhild was perusing a flower catalog.

It was a little surprising.

Brunhild had said that just as the fruit of the Norvelland Empire were inferior to the fruit of Eden, the flowers of this land were also poor quality compared to the flowers of Eden. That some nights past, she had complained that the scents filling the flower garden gave her heartburn, and she couldn't stand it. So for her to be looking at a flower catalog...

But that sort of thing didn't matter now.

Sigurd didn't give Brunhild the time to say anything—he grabbed the wrist of her left arm and drew her toward him.

"What's going on, Sigurd?"

"Just come with me."

Sigurd took Brunhild's hand, and they headed out of the estate. Their destination was the city of Nibelungen.

Time had passed since the dragons' assault, but the city was still on high alert.

Armored vehicles dotted the street, and armed soldiers were constantly on patrol.

But it was also a fact that the city was starting to regain some of its former liveliness.

The opera was starting to put on more performances, and children could be seen playing in the square with the dragonslayer statue, though their parents were not far. In his youth, Sigurd had also played dragonslayer in this square. There were customers standing and reading at the bookstore, and the stores were grilling and selling dragon meat.

"Hey, Sigurd..." Still being drawn by the hand, Brunhild kept her eyes to the ground as she walked. "I don't know what you're thinking...but let's go back. I don't want to walk through this city."

"Because it's full of dragonslayers, right?" *I know that.*

"If you were aware of how I would feel, then why did you bring me here? To harass me?"

"Maybe, yeah." He came to a stop and turned to Brunhild. "What I'm about to say will probably hurt you."

Brunhild's gaze was still on the ground.

"But I have to say it. Because you're only honest with me. Only I know what you've done. In exchange, I'll be honest with you, too. It's not an incredible secret like yours...but I'd be grateful if you kept it a secret from everyone."

He knew Brunhild planned to set a trap for their father at the conferment ceremony, and that he wouldn't be able to stop her. Of course, he would do what he could, but the odds that he could achieve the outcome he desired were slim.

If she succeeded in killing their father, then she would either flee the country, or be satisfied at having fulfilled her goal and take her own life, or be captured by the military and executed. And in the event that she failed…it went without saying.

This was his last chance to lay bare how he really felt.

"To be perfectly honest… I don't really like my father."

For the first time since coming into the city, Brunhild lifted her head. She gave Sigurd a questioning look.

"Father…doesn't think much of me. He gave the rank of second lieutenant to a woman who showed up out of nowhere, after all. It really pissed me off."

"But," he continued, "look at this city, Brunhild. I understand that it's filled with things you don't like. Like dragon meat, or dragon fat as fuel, or Eden's ashes. To you, it all must be unbearable to look at. But…"

…*they're all alive.*

"In this country, the resources from Eden allow everyone to live. Father's conquest of the Edens brings everyone happiness."

He continued, "That's why I respect him. He's hard to please, and I don't really understand him…and most of all, he did kill your father… But he's an amazing person who supports this country…and its people."

That's why I want to be like him.

Sigurd was scared. He'd probably never been this scared his whole life.

"This is…how I really feel. You can hate me if you want. It's only natural that you would, hearing this. But if this is the end…I didn't want to hide anything from a friend."

Brunhild didn't respond for a while. She was quiet, as if ruminating on Sigurd's words.

Many people passed by the two of them as they stood there in the street.

"I…" After a long pause, Brunhild began to quietly speak. "I can speak in what's known as the True Language. It allows me to communicate with any living thing without even making a sound, conveying exactly what I want to convey. It is the ultimate language."

Sigurd didn't know what this was about, but he didn't cut her off.

"Your language, on the other hand, is completely nonsensical. You say something that would hurt me terribly. I don't know what you want from me, exposing such thoughts to me. It's unclear what you're trying to get across, too. As a language, it's the worst of the worst."

Sigurd was still clasping Brunhild's hand. His hand was sweating from anxiety. But she didn't make to shake off his hand.

"Your language makes no sense at all... So why...do I...?"

The girl was actually squeezing his hand back a little harder.

Her words grew more and more heated.

"If you wish to blame me, then go right ahead. You should blame me. I've killed dozens of citizens. I've hurt hundreds. I've trampled all over your dream, too. Forget about me. Hate me. Despise me. Curse me. Strike me. That's how it should be, right? So why...? Why do you..."

...look at me with those eyes?

"I was happy."

His eyes held no anger or hatred. Unable to look him in the eye, she hung her head.

"When you told me in your sickroom about how you attacked the city, I felt like I could never forgive you, and I was angry. But I was also happy, too... I was happy you didn't disregard me, as if it was none of my business... In that moment, all was forgiven in my head. As it turns out, I'm a pretty awful guy, too."

"What you're saying is absurd... You know that, right?"

"I do."

If...

If she could lean on him.

Perhaps their future was brighter than she thought.

With Sigurd holding her hand, she could go many places. He could teach her about all the sights she would have never seen in Eden. The friendly feelings that lived within him would keep him from ever lying to her. To the girl, the boy might become a place of rest, instead of Eden.

And that thing...or rather, *Sachs*, was not completely useless. He was good at lies and putting on a public face, so the girl didn't really like him much. But she understood, at least, that the fatherly love he felt for her did not come from malice. Even if she couldn't like him as much as Sigurd, she didn't hate him. Just as Sachs had said when they'd first met in her hospital room...

It wasn't as if everyone in the world was an enemy.

If she could have taken one step...

and then another toward him...

She looked at him.

His face entered her frame of view—his large eyes, with their wide irises. And...

his black hair.

Jet-black.

The same color as that man's...

That moment.

Two memories came rushing back.

The crying dragon's corpse.

The eyes watching that expressionlessly.

The man with jet-black hair.

Suddenly, black flames blazed up inside her. The hellfire instantly burned away the warm future that had risen to her mind just a moment ago.

...I swore.

Four years ago, when she had found out that dragons had no allies in this world...

...that I would be the sole person on your side until the very end.

How could I betray myself?

Even now that her soft fantasy had melted away, the flames of hell burned fiercely within her. With that, the girl understood. In the end, the fantasy she'd been having would just get swallowed by blazing flames.

What is my purpose?

Is it to play friends with humans?

Is it to heal the wounds of my heart?

Is it to become happy?

Is it to live?

No. No to all of those.

She remembered.

The reason she had drank the blood of her beloved in order to survive.

She returned to her path.

I won't let it be the same.

The same as that hateful story.

Brunhild...no, the daughter of the dragon said...

"It's too late. It's far too late."

Her eyes no longer wavered.

"If, during the four days when I first came to this city, I had met someone kind, then perhaps I might have been able to choose a different path. But that's not how things played out.

"That's all it is," she declared coldly...

And then finally, the daughter of the dragon shook away the boy's hand.

Turning her back to him, she returned to the estate.

All he could do was watch her go.

From the start, his only goal in dragging her out to the city that day was to tell her how he really felt.

The girl was swallowed up by the crowd, and the boy could no longer see her.

Chapter

4

The sun shone in the clear blue sky on the day of the conferment ceremony.

Politicians, high officials from the military, and civilians were all in attendance. From the army up to the rank of admiral had come.

Reporters from prominent domestic newspapers were lying in wait with tons of cameras.

The stage constructed in the square was strung with red horizontal banners and large military flags that fluttered in the wind.

Chairs were fanned out in front of the stage. The seats were all filled with civilians, enough that there were also standing spectators.

Behind the wooden stage, Brunhild was waiting.

She was wearing an even fancier military uniform than normal. It was a ceremonial uniform sewn just for this occasion. Her silver hair gave her an air of class, like royalty. Other soldiers were going to be conferred honors as well, but Brunhild stood out among them.

The beautiful dragonslayer's expression was despondent.

Colonel Sachs, standing at her side, was unable to hide his irritation. "That bastard…"

Commodore Sigebert had yet to arrive.

Sachs had made him promise he would come to the capital for his daughter's conferment ceremony, at least. Sigebert had said that, after his expedition had ended, he was going to invade another ocean, so they had even adjusted the schedule for him.

But despite that, even now that it was ten minutes to the start of the event, Sigebert was nowhere to be seen.

Sigurd was lost among the crowds of civilians.

That day, the only people who could go up onstage aside from the ones receiving the honors were high officers.

"Hey…"

A voice came from behind.

He turned around to see those beady eyes.

"Father…"

Sigebert was looking at Sigurd without a word.

Sigurd was also unable to say anything.

Should he tip him off? Should he tell him that Brunhild was after his life?

Or should he hurry him onto the stage?

Those few seconds felt like an eternity. The sounds of the crowd seemed to grow distant.

In the end, Sigurd just said, "You're being targeted, Father. You can't go up onstage."

If there was any moment when father and son could have understood each other, surely, it would be right now.

"I know. I've known ever since I first saw her…," Sigebert went on. He spoke his thoughts plainly. "…She's a fearsome woman. She good at manipulating people… Sigurd, you must not let her move you."

His warning was both definitively correct and certainly wrong.

"I heard that of the dragons that attacked the capital, she failed to finish off ten white dragons. And we have yet to hunt them down. Her father… was also a white dragon."

"With silver scales and blue eyes," Sigebert muttered.

Sigebert fixed his gaze on his son and said, "I'm…sorry."

This was the first time he had spoken words of apology to his son.

"…What are you saying, Father?"

Sigebert had difficulty finding the words. But he sensed that if he let this chance go by, he likely wouldn't have another chance to speak with his son.

Among the heroes of old, there were some who had been able to intuit their coming deaths.

The premonition that Sigebert felt right now was surely of the same sort. He didn't know why, but he felt that this was likely the last time he would see his son. That was why he had sought him out.

"I had thought that once all the Edens were occupied…the dragon-slayers would no longer be needed… But I didn't make it in time. You ended up inheriting it anyway. One day, your body will also…"

Sigurd shook his head.

"That's fine. I knew when I claimed the power."

He had gotten the explanation from Sachs beforehand that Balmung would cause his body to deteriorate. But he had decided to become a dragonslayer anyway. He wanted to be someone like his father, who could support the city of Nibelungen, and he was also determined to stop his almighty friend.

Sigebert looked at the stage out of the corner of his eye. "She's going to make a move on me during this ceremony. I have no proof of this, but…"

"So you're going to catch her then."

"No. I'm going to end her."

"End her…? You mean…you're going to kill her?" he asked.

Hearing his son's tone of voice, a thought occurred to Sigebert.

Sigurd also cared deeply for her.

But there was something definitively different between Sigurd and Sachs.

It seemed that Sigurd knew her true character yet still cared for her.

Originally speaking, Sigebert's plan had been to kill the dragon's daughter with Sigurd. That was why he'd had him inherit Balmung. But he hadn't been manipulated into caring for her. His feelings were genuine.

The only one who could kill that was…

…

If at least, in the end, he could do something fatherly.

"I've always been a bad father. No, even now…"

He wasn't going to pretend to be a good father at this point.

Sigebert placed his right hand at the base of his son's neck. There was the crackle of something bursting, and Sigurd's eyes widened. A glow like a slight electric current had flowed between his right hand and Sigurd's neck, but it was barely visible under the light of the sun.

Right before passing out, his friend's face flashed through his mind, but there was nothing he could do.

Sigebert summoned a nearby soldier, entrusted him with his unconscious son, and ordered him brought to the estate.

The military band blew their horns. The conferment ceremony had begun. The explosion of sound made the civilians jump. Next, the rumble of drums rang out.

The reporters' cameras flashed one after another.

The recipients of the honors, Brunhild included, and the prime minister, who would be presenting them, made their way to the stage.

She's going to kill me.

Even if she was his son's sister.

She was a dragon, not a human.

So Sigebert made his way to the stage as well.

Because she was the main event for the ceremony, Brunhild was the last to be honored.

When Sigebert showed up after the ceremony began, Sachs cursed under his breath. But though he complained, he also smiled. "I knew he'd come."

"…You run, too," Sigebert said, even knowing it wouldn't work. But it seemed Sachs had no idea what he was talking about.

But Sigebert had the right of it.

Only Sigebert had witnessed the flames of hatred in Brunhild's eyes, and to Sachs, Brunhild was nothing more than the tragic dragonslayer.

He knew the tragic truth. If you lacked the ability to convince others, there was no point in trying.

Sigebert's words were powerless.

When Sigebert got up onstage, a storm of applause erupted from the crowd.

A girl with silver hair was standing there.

With the Silver Honor of Balmung in hand, Sigebert walked up to Brunhild.

Brunhild was gazing at Sigebert—pasting on a charming smile.

She had both hands behind her back.

She was hiding something. A weapon?

The girl's hand moved. She unfolded her hands from behind her back and thrust them out toward him.

But what she was hiding was a bouquet of flowers…

Flowers of every hue, decorated with wrapping paper and a ribbon.

It was a pleasant surprise from a daughter, arranged for her father, when she was to be presented with her medal at the ceremony. The sounds of the military band swelled.

What a miserable act.

The two of them came closer, until they were close enough that he could give her the medal, close enough that she could hand over the bouquet.

Brunhild offered the flowers…

…and with the Silver Honor of Balmung in his hand, Sigebert said,

"What a disgusting woman."

Without even lowering his voice.

But it was only the two of them at center stage, and the audience was welling with cheers, and the band was playing loudly.

So only Brunhild, who was right beside him, could hear what he said.

"I can't even believe you're my daughter."

"Accept it. Unfortunately, you and I are father and child," Brunhild said, smiling. "I…am not a dragon. I am hopelessly human. No matter how I think back on my father's words…"

<*You must not let the fires of hatred burn within you. Remember,*

even if we meet an untimely end in this life, so long as our hearts are pure, we will meet again in the Kingdom of Eternity.>

"Even when I think back on them...telling myself that doesn't work. I can't hold back the flames that burn within me."

"I..."

With that, Brunhild embraced Sigebert.

The flower bouquet fell onto the stage.

The girl brought her hands behind his neck. She wrapped her arms around the man who was a head taller than herself.

The audience cheered with joy.

It was the image of an emotional daughter embracing her father.

Though Sigebert did not return the gesture.

"I want to kill you."

The concentrated killing intent in her voice sounded like a singer's crooning of love.

She had not embraced him.

Only the two of them realized this.

Brunhild was restraining Sigebert. He tried to shake off her arms, but with her inhuman might, strong though he was, he could not immediately shake her off.

The flower bouquet...

...made a heavy thudding sound as it hit the stage.

Faintly visible between the flowers was a bent fuse.

The fuse was connected to a plastic explosive. The inside of the fuse had a firing pin on a spring. The firing pin operated and hit the detonator...hard.

The flowers scattered, flying everywhere.

In the center of the stage, the wooden floor cracked.

A dark-red gout of flames went up, swallowing the audience.

In the explosion, the other honor recipients on the stage as well as the prime minister and everyone else were torn to pieces and blasted away. The audience stationed near the stage was enveloped in the flames. Those farther away were pierced by the wooden fragments flying out at high speeds or crushed by the rocks.

The damage had been wrought by an explosive typically used for the sabotage of bridges and railways. Brunhild had procured it from the army's weapon stores and stuffed it into a bouquet.

Blood and fat splattered the shocked faces of surviving spectators. Choking dust obscured the view of the stage.

Being the closest to the bouquet, Sigebert and Brunhild could not have been expected to survive.

…That is, if the two of them had been normal humans.

"So…you've finally exposed yourself."

A dark figure swayed beyond the flames of the explosion.

Sigebert was fine.

Although the uniform he wore was torn here and there from the explosion, there was hardly any damage to his body.

His beady eyes were glaring into the air above.

Brunhild, her uniform also torn, was in the sky. The right half of her body was exposed. The scales only covered her right hand from the wrist. She was flying with a wing sprouted from the back of her right hand.

"—!"

The girl's face twisted. Even with an explosion that had enough force to destroy a bridge, all she'd been able to give Sigebert were minor cuts.

Sigebert had taken Balmung—the power of God—into his body. So at this point, his body was less that of a man and closer to that of an angel or a god. Gods' and angels' bodies were composed of a substance called ether, and there was no substance in the human realm that could damage ether. Even if Brunhild's attack had not been a bomb but a tank's cannon fire, Sigebert would have survived unscathed.

The dragon's daughter flipped around in midair. She turned away from Sigebert and attempted to flee.

"…Wait. You're the star of this ceremony." Sigebert held up his right hand. A crackling of shining energy gathered in his palm.

Lightning.

The lightning that had once slammed the first dragon, Lucifer, down into hell.

It formed the shape of a spear.

"I'll make sure you die here… I can't have you using your glib tongue to get away again."

There was the crunch of boots on earth.

A muscular right arm wound up, and he stepped forward to throw the lightning spear.

The lightning of God flew at light speed and scorched the dragon girl's back.

He heard a faint, high-pitched shriek.

Her small body, wreathed in flames, fell to the earth, however…

She's not dead yet… I didn't sense her death…

Even Sigebert Siegfried wasn't able to handle God's power perfectly. No…so long as you were human, you wouldn't be able to understand God's power. If you could, you would no longer be a human, but a god yourself.

So he used optical lenses and electronic devices to adjust the sights, condensing and releasing it. This was what the world knew as the Balmung Cannon. Without going through the cannon, the thunder would lose force and precision.

Sigebert's feet, clad in black military boots, floated off the ground.

God could fly through the air even without wings.

For Sigebert, who had the same type of power, flight was trivial.

Sigebert rose into the air, looking down from above to catch sight of multiple white shadows. They appeared suddenly, as if they had been born from the crowds.

They were midsize white dragons. Sigebert readied himself, thinking for an instant that they would attack him…

…but the white dragons scattered in all directions. East, west, south, north.

Their target was not him…but civilians.

If you were a soldier with the order to protect the people of the nation, your first priority was to protect the people. However…

"Nice try. I won't be distracted."

Sigebert was not a kind man like Sachs or Sigurd. He would strike down the source of all these evils, even if it meant allowing a few sacrifices.

Without so much as glancing in the direction of the scattered dragons,

Sigebert cut through the air, heading for the place where the dragon's daughter had fallen.

She fell over a large park in Nibelungen. It was surrounded by trees, and many of them were on fire. The flames that wreathed the girl after she had been struck by lightning had transferred to them.

Right as Sigebert approached the dragon's daughter, there was the crackling sound of something bursting.

The ground swelled up, and then a moment later, the trees were blasted away, roots and all.

With a groan, a giant silver dragon appeared.

However, from the redness of its eyes, Sigebert Siegfried knew it was her.

With the golden lightning in his right palm…

…the dragonslayer lunged at the silver dragon.

The sound of the bouquet bomb didn't reach the unconscious Sigurd's ears.

But even so, he awoke—perhaps out of a strong desire to help his friend.

Just as they were leaving the venue, he regained consciousness. Figuring out that he had been knocked out by his father's lightning, he shook off the arm of the soldier who had been trying to take him back to the estate.

Ngh… Where's Brunhild…?

Just as he thought that, the white dragons appeared.

For better or for worse, after the earlier attack, the city was in a state of special alert. The streets were dotted with armored vehicles, and they immediately went to deal with the white dragons. The civilians also began swiftly evacuating into the buildings and the subway, but there was one old man who was slow to flee.

"H…help…"

A white dragon knocked over the old man. With its sharp-clawed leg, it pushed the old man to his face and held him still, then started to tear at the flesh of his back.

Sigurd wanted to go search for Brunhild right away…

"…Dammit!"

…but he wasn't able to abandon the person being attacked before his eyes.

Sigurd Siegfried clenched his right fist. White sparks scattered around it.

All right… I can use it, too.

He gathered sparks and clenched, then threw a punch at the white dragon. In terms of both precision and force, it was still far from what his father could do, but it was enough to defeat the scaled beast.

The white dragon let out a final cry like a honking goose and crumbled, then died.

Sigurd ran up to the old man the white dragon had been attacking. He had been bitten by the dragon and was bleeding, but if he was taken to the hospital right away, he would live.

Sigurd asked a nearby middle-aged man to carry the injured man to the hospital for him. Though the suddenness of it just about made the man lose his head, he got a handle on the situation quickly and gave a sharp nod.

I heard there were ten white dragons…

It was just as expected.

A dragon that looked the same as the one he had just killed flew right in front of him. And then it started attacking someone new.

I've got to settle this fast…!

With sparks of lightning wreathing his right fist, Sigurd faced off against the new white dragon.

The park should have been rich with green, but now it was a burning sea of red.

The fire the red-eyed dragon belched and the lightning the dragonslayer flung were setting the trees and plants ablaze.

With a cry that made the air tremble, the dragon bared her claws. Capable of moving freely through the air, the dragonslayer turned aside deftly. Next, she attacked with a stomp that seemed like it would break through the earth's crust, but Sigebert evaded that, as well.

Taking advantage of the opening made after a thick leg swiped air, the dragonslayer fired his thunder.

The red-eyed dragon shrieked.

…What a pain.

Siegfried had already fired his lightning eight times. Each individual strike had enough power to kill a great dragon in an instant, but the red-eyed dragon tanked every blow.

It must be because her blood is not purely that of a dragon…not to mention that she shares my blood, too.

Lightning was a weapon that was particularly effective on dragons. But the enemy before him was only half dragon, so the effectivity of his attacks was around half of what they should've been.

In addition, since she had the blood of the dragonslayer, which was resistant against God's power, the force of his attacks was decreased even further—probably to about one-tenth.

"You know, I'm not particularly interested in going toe to toe with a dragon."

But he refused to lose.

It would take time to kill her. That was all.

He ducked through both pairs of the dragon's legs. As he was passing by, he used his palm to strike deep into a left leg. The dragon cried out in pain.

"So help me out here. If you stop resisting, I can promise a quick and painless death."

But the red-eyed dragon continued to struggle.

She knew she had no chance of winning.

She was in a hopeless position, flailing her limbs about wildly.

For the first time in a long time, she looked like the child she truly was.

The battle-hardened dragonslayer was cautious.

She wouldn't be able to rage around recklessly forever. She would run out of strength soon. While maintaining a distance from the dragon's claws and flames, he would look for his chance to strike at her body with his lightning.

Although he was at a loss for how to continue his offensive, the dragonslayer's victory was all but assured.

Was it a coincidence that the newborn dragonslayer came to that park? Thinking about it now, the white dragons had shown no signs of resistance toward the new dragonslayer, not even once. They just kept showing up in front of him and attacking civilians. Even if Sigurd beat one and continued his search for Brunhild, the next dragon would immediately show up and attack another human. So Sigurd was forced to go after them. This happened again and again.

If there was someone controlling the white dragons, then surely they would know…

…that unlike *her*, the boy was a kind person.

That if someone was being attacked, he would be unable to abandon them.

Just as he dealt a killing blow to another white dragon, a giant silver dragon and his father, facing off against it, caught his eye. Even Sigurd could tell that his father was at a loss for how to attack.

Silver scales…

He remembered his father's words at the event venue.

The dragon his father was fighting now was covered in silver scales.

So this is the boss of the white dragons…!

He clenched his lightning fist.

It was only natural for him to assume it was the dragons' boss.

In the story that Brunhild had recounted to him in the hospital room, there had been a part about her turning humans into dragons…

But she hadn't mentioned anything about becoming a dragon herself.

He clenched his fists hard, even harder.

He condensed his lightning so he could kill it in one strike. The silver dragon was distracted by his father and didn't even notice him. He would finish it off by attacking its blind spot.

It would take about ten seconds, but Sigurd clenched the maximum amount of lightning that he could handle.

And then the dragonslayer fired it…

Balmung.

The dragonslayer hadn't noticed. This was partially because he was focused on concentrating his lightning. But after firing it, he noticed, and remembered.

His father had said…

It had silver scales and blue eyes.

But the dragon that was trying to kill his father now…

…had the red eyes he knew so well.

Did the dragon *truly* never notice the boy?

Despite how it had been flailing about in desperation thus far, this one motion was fluid.

The dragon that was silver with red eyes snatched up Sigebert Siegfried with its right hand…

…and used his body as a shield for the Balmung shot that the boy fired.

Sigebert Siegfried's body was largely made of ether. It couldn't be injured by human weapons or a dragon's power.

But if it was the lightning of Balmung…

Lightning was God's weapon. It was comprised of the same substance as ether.

After only getting scrapes until this point, Sigebert's body was hit with all the lightning the boy had concentrated, and his flesh was burned to a crisp in the blink of an eye. He likely hadn't even had time to process what had happened.

Even Sigurd could not immediately comprehend what had happened.

The dragon's right arm that had been clutching Sigebert, as well as the upper right portion of its body, were annihilated along with the father.

There were scrapes and wounds all over the dragon's body. Blood flowed like a waterfall, not a like mercury, but a dark-red mucus.

The silver dragon inspected herself.

She did not fear death.

In the boy's head, she was beyond all that.

His recalled his conversation with the red-eyed girl.

Once, she said this to me.

Turning her face away from me, with her small shoulders trembling.

"I'm sorry."

Was this what she meant?

She literally couldn't kill their father, so she would have his son do it for her... Was that why she had apologized?

Had she been expressing remorse for forcing him to take on the sin of patricide?

The red-eyed white dragon swayed.

Her long neck slammed into the burning grasses.

The dragon's head was right in front of Sigurd.

"Y...you..."

The boy called to her.

"Was this...your plan...all along...?" he asked.

There was no answer.

Emotionless red eyes simply gazed at him.

"Say something..."

She said nothing.

"I'm the one person you'll be honest with...right?"

But she still said nothing.

Then the boy finally realized... It wasn't that the dragon wouldn't speak. She couldn't.

Of course there was no emotion in her bloodred eyes. By the time she had fallen, she was already dead.

The countless holes gouged in her body had certainly brought the silver dragon closer to death...

But the final strike...

...had been Sigurd's Balmung, burning away the right half of her body. A red puddle gradually oozed out.

...Who had ever been able to understand her?

Not Father, not the colonel, perhaps not even her own father. Not even me. Perhaps no one understood her.

That was...because they all just saw that she was abnormally smart, or very strong, or beautiful yet fragile, like glass, or a friend... Things of that nature. When the truth was...

Those eyes seemed to see through everything, but in truth they only ever saw one person. And despite being smart, what she was trying to do was the height of stupidity... And despite being so strong, when I said "...I'm your

friend," she goddamn cried, and despite having a pretty, mature face, she was
a pathetic little kid on the inside.

Because she was a dragon and a human.

Because that was the kind of person she was.

Because I understood she was a pain in the ass, and hard to understand,
and a worrywart...

At the end, I was able to like her... I didn't want her to die.

I didn't want to kill her.

Having lost the two people dearest to him in an instant, just how long
did the boy stand there?

Before he knew it, the flames were extinguished, and there were people
gathered around him and the corpses.

One of the people said,

"He's a dragonslayer."

Then someone else said,

"The dragonslayer protected us."

Cheers and applause welled up.

The people gave words of thanks, but it all sounded like it came from
a distant world to him.

The title that the boy had once desired rang hollow in his head.

Epilogue

Powerful rain battered the hut.

Even now that the girl had finished her story, the long night showed no sign of ending.

Her once-soaked uniform had long since dried.

The girl in a red military uniform and the man with silver hair were sitting face-to-face.

The only sound that could be heard for some time was the crackling of hearth fire.

<But I told you so many times…,> the young man said bitterly. <I told you over and over that you must not harbor hatred… You must not kill in hatred.>

The girl in a red military uniform was unable to reply.

<I wished for it. I dreamed of the days I could spend with you here. I loved you.>

I did love you.

<I wanted to be with you forever. I wanted to be by your side always. Even if we have no bond of blood, I thought of myself as…>

…as your father.

<I will hate you forever. As much as I loved you, I will hate you. I will loathe you for all eternity. I hate you for leaving a void in me that will never be filled… In a land of everlasting life…>

The daughter said nothing in her own defense. There was nothing she could say.

<I will take my leave now,> the girl said, and stood up.

Outside the hut, a storm that would never end continued to rage on.

But even so, the girl had to leave.

Battered by rain that would never stop, in a storm that continued to blow, she would continue to wander incessantly through a darkness that would never see dawn.

She was not allowed to remain in the hut.

The only ones allowed to get warmth from those logs were those who had not turned their back on God's teachings.

Even if they were a silver dragon, God's teachings could not be disobeyed. He would not be able to even beg for God's mercy.

If anything, this occasion *was* God's mercy.

By all accounts, this girl should have been cast down to hell. This moment in which she was allowed to stop by this hill, and enter the hut, should have been impossible.

Since the hill where this hut stood…

…was a place the people of the mundane world called the Kingdom of Eternity.

The girl had surely been able to stop by that hut because God had taken pity on her.

She pushed with her scaleless right hand and opened the door. The wind and rain wet the floor.

The girl walked through the door that led outside.

The dragon unthinkingly stood from his chair.

We could walk through the darkness of night together. But no, I can't… If only it were allowed…

But he was not allowed to follow her.

Just as those who had fallen to hell were not worthy of rising to the Kingdom of Eternity,

the ones allowed to live in the Kingdom of Eternity were not able to fall to hell.

The silver dragon could only watch her go.

<I'll say it again. I…>

His voice wavered.

<I hate you. I hate you for making me feel this way. No matter how much time it takes, no matter how many words it takes, I won't be able to convey flames of hatred that burn in my heart. I will continue to hate for the rest of eternity... But still...>

When he continued...

A gemlike teardrop fell.

<Thank you.>

For fighting for me,
For raging for me,
For hating for me,
For rampaging for me,
For...

...feeling that much for me.

He could hear the sound of sniffling.

The girl in the military uniform didn't turn around.

It's not like that.
It was, but it wasn't.
It was true that I only ever thought of you.
I love you.

Even now, this feeling...
It's not some resplendent jewel.
It's something that makes me want to lock you up in a cage, kill everyone who gets in my way, monopolize you so no one else can see you, toy with you, violate you, devour you until there isn't a single scrap of flesh left—
It's a selfish, black, ugly feeling.
I am no martyr.

For an instant, the girl thought about confessing these thoughts, too. After talking this much about her own acts of brutality, it still didn't seem like something to hide.

But.

Even if it was far too late now, and there was no taking anything back, and she couldn't smooth anything over.

Without turning back,

without ever turning back, the girl said this.

<With only those **two words**, I feel like I can walk through the never-ending darkness forever.>

Just a little was fine.

If even the tiniest portion of his memory of her could remain unblemished, that was enough.

The dragon's daughter left the hut.

The silver dragon followed after her, but the strong wind prevented him from getting outside.

The door was slammed shut with a loud bang.

After the girl was out of sight, dawn finally arrived.

The sun rose above a bright-blue sky.

The gloom the girl vanished into had disappeared from the hut.

Afterword

I love stories about love and justice.

I want bad people to lose, and I want the hardworking to be rewarded.

Those thinking *Hey, hey, hey, hold on. How can you say that?* must have read *Brunhild the Dragonslayer* until the end. Thank you very much.

Next, I assume you will say this:

"Someone who likes love and justice wouldn't write a story with an ending like this."

It's natural to think so. But that's not quite true.

At the stage when I started writing *Brunhild the Dragonslayer*, it was a completely different story.

No one was supposed to die. Brunhild is torn away from the silver dragon, but they weren't parted by death. The conquest of Eden by Brunhild's blood father, Sigebert, led to the silver dragon's disappearance, but the truth was that Sigebert was very kind (though the current Sigebert is also kind) and takes the silver dragon into his protection. After reconciling with Sigebert, Brunhild goes to see the silver dragon, who is living hidden deep in the mountains. I think that was basically the story.

So I did start writing it as a story of love and justice. I always start writing with that sort of motive.

But whenever I write, *they* always appear.

That is to say, the other me. They look down at my draft and whisper in my ear.

Hey, that's not right. Things wouldn't go that well, would they? Do you really believe that the world is overflowing with love and justice?

Maybe the me that whispers this is the real me. Not only is this whisper extremely sweet, it's intense, and what I write rapidly pulls away from love and justice. For a while there, I completely lost to the whispers, and there was even a time when I gave into it.

But I started to want to struggle.

It was ever since I encountered a certain book and saw that author fighting.

So this time, I absolutely do not want to give in.

I struggled on with no regard to appearances. I couldn't be picky about my methods. I believe that is expressed in Brunhild's struggle. The various threats who attack her in the book are all assassins set on her by the other me in order to kill her. At the point where I wrote the assassins, I wasn't thinking about the ways in which she would defeat them. So Brunhild and I thought of a way to win together. Normally, I lose to the whispers, but this time, my thoughts wouldn't stop.

The result was the ending you read.

Perhaps it's an awful story. It might not be a story of love and justice. Maybe the bad guys didn't lose, and those who tried their hardest weren't rewarded. I have no intention of denying such opinions.

But this is the story I can be proud of. It's an award winner, after all.

Lastly, I offer my undying thanks to A, who does much at Dengeki Bunko, and who gave me the motive to write this book.